TOP COW PRODUCTIONS PRESENTS

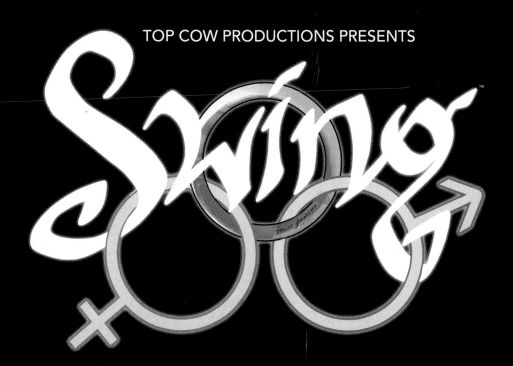

Created by

LINDA SEJIC, MATT HAWKINS & JENNI CHEUNG

Published by Top Cow Productions, Inc.
Los Angeles

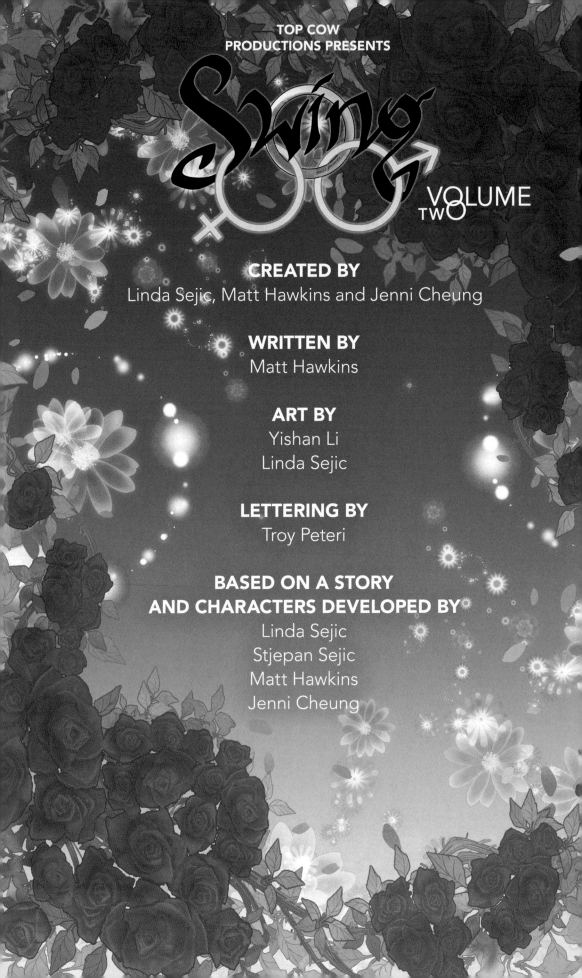

TOP COW
PRODUCTIONS PRESENTS

Swing

VOLUME TWO

CREATED BY
Linda Sejic, Matt Hawkins and Jenni Cheung

WRITTEN BY
Matt Hawkins

ART BY
Yishan Li
Linda Sejic

LETTERING BY
Troy Peteri

**BASED ON A STORY
AND CHARACTERS DEVELOPED BY**
Linda Sejic
Stjepan Sejic
Matt Hawkins
Jenni Cheung

CAST

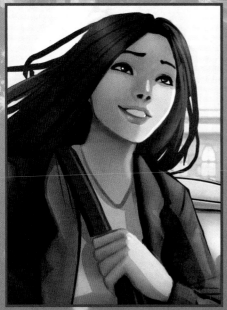

Cathy Chang

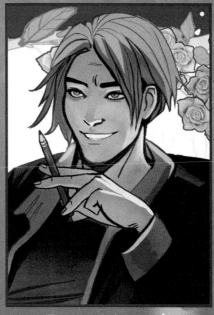

Dan Lincoln

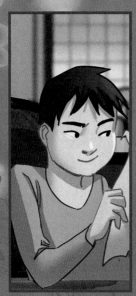

Blake Lincoln

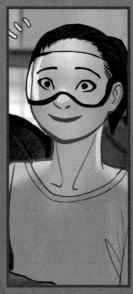

Ashley Lincoln

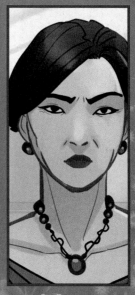

Mom

IMAGE COMICS, INC.

Robert Kirkman—Chief Operating Officer
Erik Larsen—Chief Financial Officer
Todd McFarlane—President
Marc Silvestri—Chief Executive Officer
Jim Valentino—Vice President
Eric Stephenson—Publisher/Chief Creative Officer
Jeff Boison—Director of Publishing Planning & Book Trade Sales
Chris Ross—Director of Digital Sales
Jeff Stang—Director of Direct Market Sales
Kat Salazar—Director of PR & Marketing
Drew Gill—Art Director
Heather Doornink—Production Director
Nicole Lapalme—Controller
IMAGECOMICS.COM

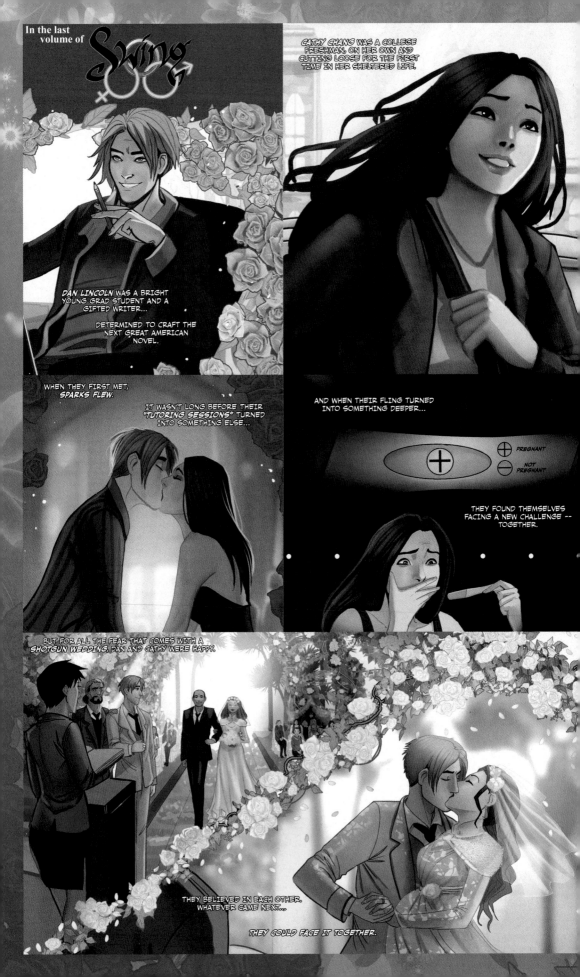

In the last volume of *Swing*

CATHY CHANG WAS A COLLEGE FRESHMAN, ON HER OWN AND CUTTING LOOSE FOR THE FIRST TIME IN HER SHELTERED LIFE.

DAN LINCOLN WAS A BRIGHT YOUNG GRAD STUDENT AND A GIFTED WRITER...

DETERMINED TO CRAFT THE NEXT GREAT AMERICAN NOVEL.

WHEN THEY FIRST MET, *SPARKS FLEW.*

IT WASN'T LONG BEFORE THEIR *"TUTORING SESSIONS"* TURNED INTO SOMETHING ELSE...

AND WHEN THEIR FLING TURNED INTO SOMETHING DEEPER...

PREGNANT

NOT PREGNANT

THEY FOUND THEMSELVES FACING A NEW CHALLENGE -- TOGETHER.

BUT FOR ALL THE FEAR THAT COMES WITH A SHOTGUN WEDDING, DAN AND CATHY WERE HAPPY.

THEY BELIEVED IN EACH OTHER. WHATEVER CAME NEXT...

THEY COULD FACE IT TOGETHER.

BUT *8 YEARS* AND *TWO KIDS* LATER,
THE MAGIC STARTED TO FADE.

ROUTINE REPLACED ROMANCE.

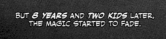

RESPONSIBILITY

DAN STARTED *TEACHING* HIGH
SCHOOL ENGLISH --

AND SPENT MORE TIME
GRINDING AWAY AT RPGS THAN
WRITING HIS NOVEL.

CATHY ENDED UP IN THE
ENTERTAINMENT INDUSTRY --

COURTING CLIENTS AND
MANAGING A TEAM OF WEB
DESIGNERS AND ENGINEERS.

THE MORE THEY DRIFTED, THE
MORE *TEMPTATION* LOOMED.

BUT THEY LOVED EACH OTHER.

THEY DIDN'T WANT TO FEEL THIS
RESENTMENT.

THEY BOTH WANTED TO FEEL
CLOSER...

THEY WOULD BECOME *SWINGERS.*

THEY WANTED TO FEEL
THE HEAT AGAIN.

AND CATHY HAD A PLAN TO PUT
THE SPICE BACK INTO THEIR
MARRIAGE.

I THINK I'D LIKE
TO TRY THAT.

THEY MADE RULES. THEY RESPECTED EACH OTHER'S BOUNDARIES.
AND AT FIRST, MERELY ENTERTAINING THE IDEA SEEMED TO BRING BACK THE OLD EXCITEMENT.
WHAT THE FUCK?
BUT DAN WAS SKEPTICAL AND INSECURE.
CATHY WAS PATIENT...
BUT SHE WORRIED THEIR MARRIAGE WAS ENDING BEFORE THEY COULD EVEN TRY OPENING IT UP.
SHE CONFIDED IN AN OLD FRIEND...
SO WITH DEBBIE'S HELP, CATHY HATCHED A PLAN.
NO STRANGERS, NO SPECIAL CLUBS --
JUST GOOD OLD-FASHIONED SEDUCTION.
IT WAS FAR FROM TRADITIONAL, BUT IT WORKED.
HERE WAS SOMETHING NEW, AND DAN AND CATHY LOVED IT.
AND LOVED EACH OTHER MORE FOR IT.
THE ONLY WORRY WAS --
COULD THEY KEEP IT UP?

WATCHING MY HUSBAND WITH ANOTHER WOMAN KIND OF TURNS ME ON.
THAT'S CALLED COMPERSION.
IT'S THE OPPOSITE OF JEALOUSY.
IT MEANS TO FEEL JOY AND EXCITEMENT WATCHING SOMEONE YOU LOVE FEEL PLEASURE... EVEN WHEN IT'S WITH SOMEONE ELSE.

LET'S SWITCH IT UP.
HER NIPPLES ARE CRAZY SENSITIVE.
OH YEAH?
YOU GO DOWN. I'LL STAY UP HERE.
SOUNDS GOOD.
I'D NEVER BEEN WITH A WOMAN BEFORE ALL THIS.

I DON'T THINK I'M BISEXUAL, BUT I'M TRYING TO KEEP AN OPEN MIND AND FULLY EXPLORE MY SEXUALITY...BUT DAN AND I DON'T SEEM TO BE IN SYNC WITH IT ALL YET.
HE SEEMS TO LIKE THIS, THOUGH.

DOCKWEILER BEACH
LOS ANGELES, CALIFORNIA.
I'M TWENTY-EIGHT YEARS OLD AND DAN IS THE ONLY MAN I'VE HAD SEX WITH.
MOST OF MY GIRLFRIENDS AREN'T EVEN MARRIED YET AND HAVE HAD MORE SEXUAL PARTNERS IN THE LAST MONTH THAN I'VE EVER HAD.
AFTER TWO KIDS AND EIGHT YEARS OF MARRIAGE, I WANTED TO SPICE UP OUR SEX LIFE, SO I CONVINCED DAN WE SHOULD TRY THIS.
SWINGING, ETHICAL NON-MONOGAMY, LIFESTYLE...WHATEVER YOU WANT TO CALL IT...IT'S HAVING SEX WITH OTHER PEOPLE WITHOUT CHEATING.
WE'RE TAKING IT SLOW AND DISCOVERING OUR BOUNDARIES.
WEREN'T THEY BOTH JUST BABIES, CATH? NOW LOOK AT THEM. BLAKE IS ALMOST AS TALL AS ASHLEY.
PRETTY SOON THEY'LL BE DATING.
OH MY GOD, I HADN'T EVEN THOUGHT ABOUT ANY OF THAT YET. I'LL KILL ANY BOY THAT EVEN LOOKS AT HER.
LET'S MAKE IT BIGGER.

DON'T SAY SHIT LIKE THAT, EVEN IN JEST.
MY MOM'S OVERBEARING ANTI-SEX MANTRA JUST MADE ME WANT TO DO IT MORE.
YEAH, YOU HO, KNOCKED UP AT EIGHTEEN.
TAKES TWO TO TANGO. I DON'T RECALL YOU PREACHING ABSTINENCE AT THE TIME.
I KNOW, I'M JUST KIDDING, BABE.
WANT TO PUT YOUR HANDS ON ME, LOVERBOY? I COULD USE SOME MORE SUNSCREEN.

I'VE STARTED WORKING ON MY BOOK AGAIN.
REALLY? WHEN'S THE LAST TIME YOU WROTE?
YEARS. I DON'T EVEN REMEMBER. I SCRAPPED WHAT I WAS DOING AND STARTED A NEW ONE ABOUT A VICTORIAN MAN WHO HAS TWO LOVERS.
INSPIRED BY BANGING ALL MY LOOSE FRIENDS?
ACTUALLY, YES.

AND I'VE BEEN MEANING TO TALK TO YOU ABOUT ALL THAT.
SECOND THOUGHTS AGAIN? WE CAN QUIT IF IT BOTHERS YOU.
NO, THAT'S NOT IT AT ALL.
THEN WHAT IS IT?
WE'VE HAD A SERIES OF THREESOMES WITH YOUR GIRLFRIENDS, IT JUST DOESN'T SEEM FAIR.
I THINK I'M READY TO TRY A COUPLE.
REALLY?

HONEY, YOUR BOOBS ARE SHOWING.
NO ONE CAN SEE, PRUDE. ARE YOU SURE YOU WANT TO DO THIS?
YEAH, LET'S DO IT. YOU'VE BEEN SO GOOD TO ME AND I HAVEN'T DEVELOPED ANY FEELINGS FOR ANYONE ELSE.
IT'LL BE DIFFERENT WITH A MAN THERE.
I KNOW, BUT NOTHING VENTURED, NOTHING GAINED.
THIS HAS REALLY INSPIRED ME CREATIVELY AND I WANT TO SEE WHERE IT LEADS.
IF WE DO EVERYTHING TOGETHER AND ARE HONEST WITH EACH OTHER, I THINK WE'LL BE OKAY.
MY BIGGEST FEAR IS THIS SPILLING INTO OUR REGULAR LIVES. I'LL WRITE UP A LIST OF RULES, BOUNDARIES, WHATEVER YOU WANT TO CALL IT, AND ONCE WE'RE AGREED ON ALL THAT, WE CAN SET UP ONE OF THOSE ONLINE PROFILES.

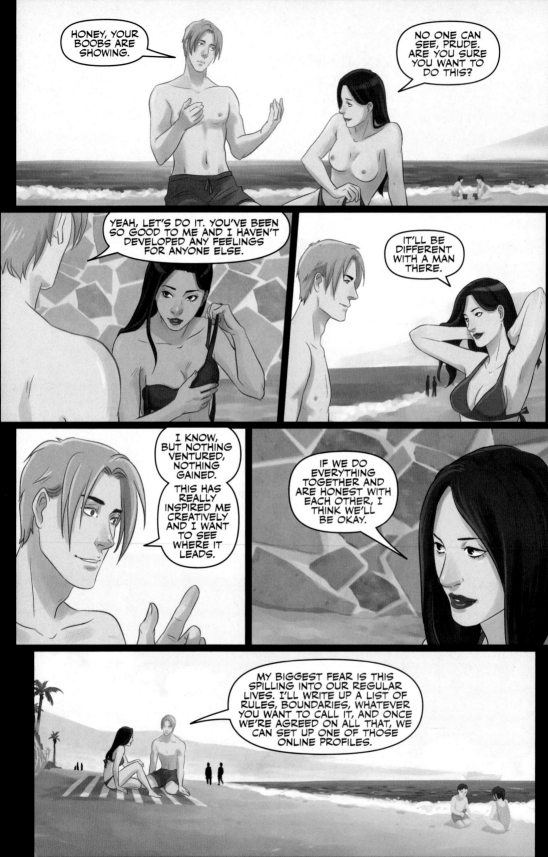

View Zoom Add Page Insert Text Shape

Rules

1) We only play together, never separately.
2) No exchanging of contact information other than the joint email and messaging app we'll be using.
3) No taking one for the team. Both of us need to be attracted to the other person.
4) No monster cock dudes.
5) Transparency and honesty in all things.
6) Condoms for any penetration (unless it's us, of course).
7) If either of us isn't into it at any point (even mid-sex) we stop and leave and promise not to be mad about it.
8) I'll do the online chatting to vet people, but I'll pretend to be you.
9) The goal is variety, so let's limit the number of times we hook up with the same couple to prevent possible emotional attachment.
10) No individual outside contact of any kind with people we've played with.

We always do our communication together. If this happens by accident (one of us runs into a play partner at the grocery store) we tell the other immediately.

THE IDEA OF CATHY HAVING SEX WITH OTHER MEN TERRIFIES ME.

I LIKED THAT I WAS THE ONLY GUY SHE'D BEEN WITH, BUT SHE WAS LUCKY NUMBER THIRTEEN FOR ME...SO I GET IT.

I AM REALLY TORN ABOUT DOING THIS, BUT IF I DON'T AT LEAST TRY SHE MIGHT RESENT ME FOR IT, NOW THAT WE'VE HAD THREESOMES WITH SOME OF HER FRIENDS.

I REALLY DON'T WANT MY PARENTS FINDING OUT ABOUT THIS. THEY LOVE CATHY AND THEY'D PROBABLY JUST ROLL THEIR EYES AT MY DOING THIS...BUT I THINK THEY'D LIKE HER LESS IF THEY FOUND OUT.

I KNOW I SHOULD BE MORE OPEN WITH HER ABOUT MY FEARS, BUT I THINK WITH THE BOUNDARIES WE'LL BE FINE. WE KEEP OUR REAL LIVES SEPARATE FROM THIS.

SO YOU WANT TO PRETEND THAT YOU'RE ME WHILE CHATTING WITH PEOPLE?
YOU THINK I'LL SAY SOMETHING STUPID?
I'M NOT WORRIED ABOUT YOU, IT'S DUDES THAT CONCERN ME. IF THE GUY SAYS SOMETHING DISRESPECTFUL OR ANYTHING EVEN REMOTELY SHADY...LIKE TRYING TO MEET UP WITH YOU WITHOUT ME...HE GETS VETOED.
ALL THESE RULES, IT SEEMS YOU DON'T REALLY WANT TO DO THIS. IF YOU DON'T THAT'S FINE, HONEY, JUST SAY SO.
I'M DOWN TO TRY.
OKAY THEN, LET'S SET UP OUR PROFILE.
WE SHOULD START ON THIS SITE AND BRANCH OUT FROM THERE.
WE NEED TO PICK A PROFILE PIC. THE FAQ SAYS IT'S IMPORTANT TO INCLUDE AT LEAST ONE CLEAR FACE AND BODY SHOT. A LOT OF PROFILES INCLUDE NUDES OR PARTIAL NUDES.

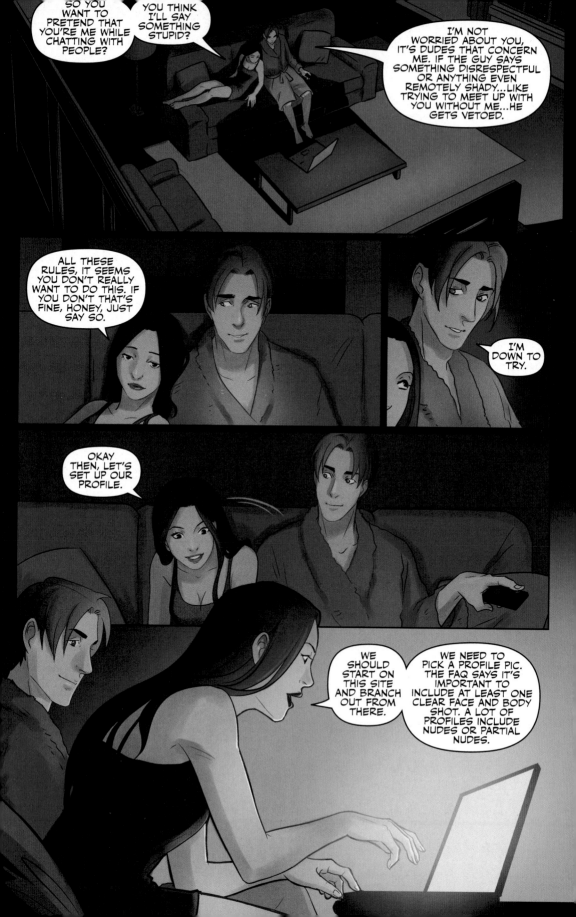

I DON'T THINK THOSE WILL WORK.
I'M DOWN FOR RACY IN THAT SPECIFIC PIC IF WE CAN'T BE IDENTIFIED.
THAT'S HOT.
WE DO LOOK GOOD NAKED.

I'M SO TURNED ON BY THE THOUGHT OF ALL THIS, I HOPE IT WORKS OUT. I REALLY WANT TO EXPLORE MY SEXUALITY.
LIFE'S TOO SHORT, AFTER ALL!
I'M STILL SCARED ABOUT HOW I'LL FEEL, BUT IF ANYTHING UNCOOL HAPPENS I CAN USE THAT AS AN EXCUSE TO STOP IT.
PLUS, OUR SEX LIFE HAS BEEN AMAZINGLY BETTER FROM JUST TALKING ABOUT ALL THIS.
I LOVE YOU, YA KNOW.
I LOVE YOU TOO, BABY CAKES.
IF WE'RE OPEN AND HONEST WITH EACH OTHER AND TALK THROUGH OUR FEELINGS, I THINK WE MIGHT ACTUALLY BE ABLE TO PULL THIS OFF.

I'M LISTING YOU AS HETEROSEXUAL AND ME AS HETERO-FLEXIBLE.
WHAT'S THAT MEAN?
TAP
THAT I'M NOT FULLY BISEXUAL, BUT I'LL PLAY WITH GIRLS.
I LIKE GIRLS WHEN I'M DRUNK.
THAT'S KIND OF HOT.
YOU'VE SEEN ME WITH GIRLS BEFORE.
AND I'D LIKE TO SEE YOU WITH MORE.
MMM.

OH!
DAN.
YEAH?
I WANT YOU INSIDE ME.

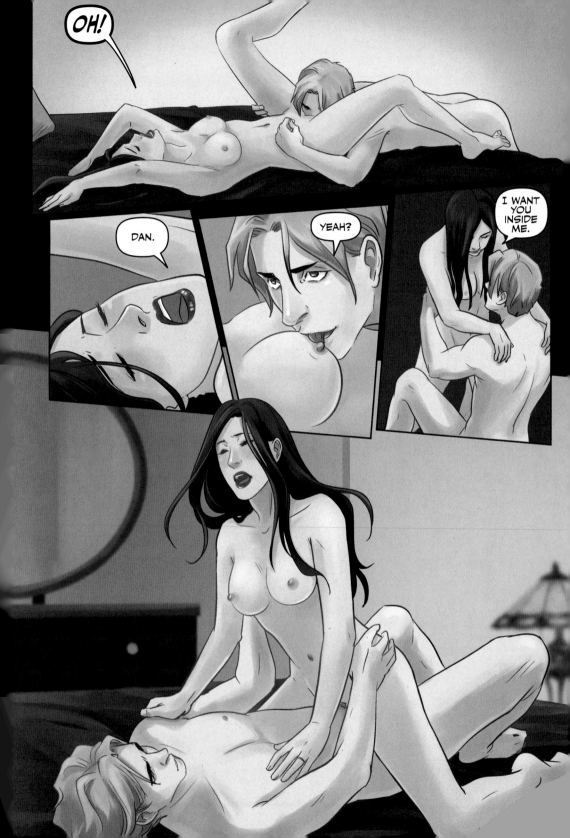

ARE WE READY TO GO LIVE WITH THE PROFILE?
YEAH, LET'S DO IT.
THE SITE HAS AN APP I'VE SET UP ON YOUR PHONE SO YOU CAN CHECK IT DURING THE DAY AND WE CAN DO IT TOGETHER FROM OUR LAPTOPS AT NIGHT.
SOUNDS GOOD.
WE ARE LIVE, STUD.
ARE YOU READY FOR A FUN ADVENTURE?
ALWAYS, AS LONG AS I'M WITH YOU.
LITTLE DID WE KNOW THE FLAKES AND FAKES THAT POPULATE THESE SITES.

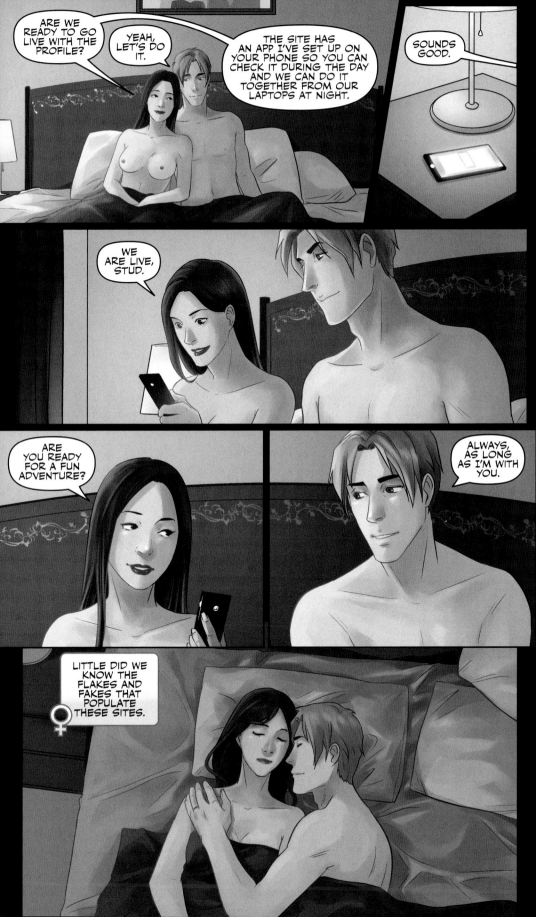

OUR FIRST FEW MEET-UPS WENT BADLY.
PEOPLE USING OLD PHOTOS.
INTERESTING ANGLES.
WE WERE TRYING NOT TO BE JUDGMENTAL...BUT COME ON.
AND THOSE ARE THE PEOPLE THAT SHOWED. *FAKES*, WE STARTED CALLING THEM.
THE *FLAKES* WERE PEOPLE WHO SET A MEET-UP AND THEN JUST GHOSTED.
IT WAS FRUSTRATING.

OUR LAST MEET-UP WAS OVER A MONTH AGO WITH A GUY WHO PRETENDED TO HAVE A WIFE AND SHOWED UP BY HIMSELF.

THAT'S HOW WE DISCOVERED THERE WERE A LOT OF SINGLE MEN WHO LIED ABOUT BEING WITH A WOMAN TO COLLECT NUDE PICS OR HOPED WE'D HAVE A THREESOME.

THERE ARE HONEST SINGLE MEN IN LIFESTYLE WHO PLAY WITH COUPLES, BOTH STRAIGHT AND BISEXUAL, BUT I KNEW DAN WOULD NOT BE INTO THAT.

CATH, WE'VE GOT A NEW MATCH. THEY LOOK GOOD... IF THEY'RE LEGIT. CHERI AND JACK.

THEY'RE CUTE... IF THEY'RE FOR REAL.

AFTER A COUPLE MONTHS I'D STARTED TO LOSE HOPE WE'D MEET ANYONE OUR SPEED.

WE FELL BACK INTO THE ROUTINES AND OUR BRIEF HOT SEX DEVOLVED BACK INTO GOING THROUGH THE MOTIONS.

I'M A LITTLE TIRED OF BEING DISAPPOINTED.

THEY WANT TO CHAT TONIGHT. AT THE VERY LEAST, MAYBE IT'LL GET US WORKED UP.

YOU MEAN TWO MINUTES?

I'LL GO DOWN ON YOU FOR LIKE TWO HOURS.

I MISSED OUT ON THE WHOLE ONLINE DATING THING SO A LOT OF THIS WAS NEW TO ME.
SO THEY'VE BEEN INTO THE LIFESTYLE FOR TEN YEARS.
SHOULD WE TELL THEM WE'RE NOOBS?
THE TRUTH IS EASIER TO REMEMBER.
STEALING MY LINES NOW?
THEY SEEM COOL. RESPECTFUL. YOU WANT TO SET A DRINK DATE?
SURE.

THIS WHOLE THING HAS MADE ME APPRECIATE DAN EVEN MORE. HE'S REAL IN A SEA OF SO MANY FAKERS.
IF THEY'RE ANOTHER ONE OF OUR FAKES OR FLAKES, I DON'T THINK I WANT TO TRY THIS ANYMORE.
LOL, very
Video Chat?
VIDEO CHAT, WHAT DO YOU THINK ABOUT THAT, MISTER SCAREDY-PANTS?
IT WOULD HELP ELIMINATE THE FAKERS. YEAH, LET'S DO IT.

HI, GUYS. I'M MARY AND THIS IS MY HUSBAND CLINT. WE USE CHERI AND JACK UNTIL WE SEE THE COUPLE'S LEGIT.
WE THOUGHT ABOUT CODE NAMES, TOO.
DAN AND CATHY ARE OUR REAL NAMES.
WE THOUGHT FAKE ONES MIGHT BE TOO HARD TO REMEMBER WHEN WE WERE DRUNK.
YOU GUYS ARE SUPER CUTE.
I HAVE A RITUAL TO DETERMINE IF WE'RE GOING TO GET ALONG, SO ANSWER ME THIS: WHAT'S THE DIFFERENCE BETWEEN A CAR TIRE AND THREE HUNDRED AND SIXTY-FIVE USED CONDOMS?
UH...
ONE'S A GOOD YEAR, THE OTHER IS A GREAT YEAR.
HAHAHA HAHAHA
LAUGHING AT MY DUMB JOKES MEANS YOU TWO ARE AWESOME.

THIS VIDEO CHAT IS A GREAT IDEA, I WISH WE'D THOUGHT OF IT. WE'VE BEEN ON SO MANY MEET AND GREETS WITH THE FAKES AND BEEN GHOSTED BY FLAKES.
THAT HAPPENED TO US A FEW TIMES TOO, SO WE USE THIS TO MAKE SURE THE COUPLE OR UNICORN IS LEGIT.
WHAT'S A UNICORN?
THAT'S A SINGLE FEMALE THAT LIKES TO HAVE SEX WITH COUPLES. THEY'RE UNICORNS BECAUSE THEY'RE RARE AND MAGICAL.
OH MY GOD, THAT'S SO FUNNY.
WE'RE NOT QUITE DOWN WITH ALL THE LINGO YET.
YEAH, HOPEFULLY THIS ISN'T A TURNOFF FOR YOU, BUT WE'VE NEVER ACTUALLY PLAYED WITH ANOTHER COUPLE. I'VE GOT SOME GIRLFRIENDS WHO WERE UP FOR SOME THREESOME FUN, BUT THAT'S AS FAR AS WE'VE GONE.
WE TEND TO AVOID NEW PEOPLE BECAUSE SOME OF THE EMOTIONAL HURDLES ARE HARD FOR SOME NEWER PEOPLE TO OVERCOME AND WE TRY TO AVOID DRAMA--
BUT YOU TWO SEEM AWESOME AND WE'D LOVE TO MEET YOU. EVEN IF WE CAN ONLY SHARE SOME WAR STORIES AND OUR EXPERIENCE, IT MIGHT HELP YOU DETERMINE IF THIS IS FOR YOU.

THAT'S REALLY VERY NICE OF YOU, THANKS FOR THAT.
YEAH, YOU TWO SEEM SUPER CHILL.
ANOTHER REASON WE LIKE THE VIDEO CHAT IS WE'RE BOTH A BIT EXHIBITIONIST.
SO FEEL FREE TO WATCH OR HANG UP, WE WON'T BE OFFENDED.

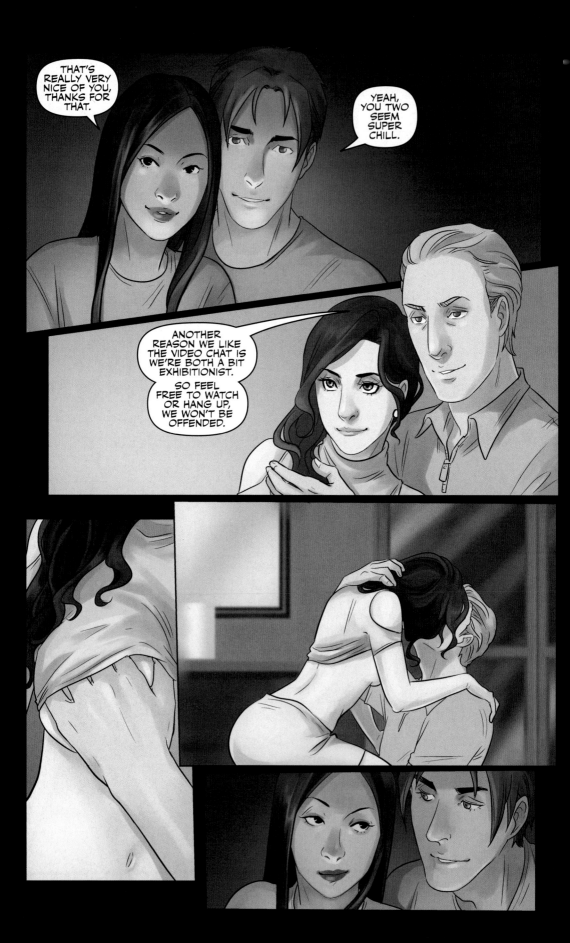

YOU'RE A LUCKY MAN, DAN. THIS IS ALL HAPPENING FAST AND I DON'T WANT TO SCARE YOU TWO OFF, SO LET'S SIGN OFF FOR NOW.
HOPEFULLY WE'LL SEE YOU SOON. HAVE A GOOD NIGHT!

OHHH!
IS MOMMY OKAY?
SHE'S FINE, HONEY, GO BACK TO BED.
YOU'RE HAVING SEX, I'M NOT DUMB. DON'T YOU HAVE YOUR OWN ROOM FOR THAT?
I WATCH TV THERE, YA KNOW.

THEY INVITED US OUT FOR DRINKS FRIDAY. I REALLY LIKE THEM.
MY MOM CAN WATCH THE KIDS.
I'M *REALLY* HOPING THIS ISN'T ANOTHER DISAPPOINTMENT.
I'VE ENJOYED OUR THREESOMES, BUT I PREFER MEN, AND IF WE DON'T GRADUATE TO FOURSOMES SOON, I'M DONE.
WHAT TIME IS IT?
THEY'VE GOT SIX MINUTES UNTIL THEY'RE *LATE.* RELAX, TEACHER MAN, NOT EVERYONE HAS A BELL SCHEDULE LIKE YOU DO IN YOUR CLASS.
HELLO THERE.

I LOVE PUNCTUAL PEOPLE.
DO YOU KNOW WHY DR. PEPPER COMES IN A BOTTLE?
WHAT?
IT'S BECAUSE HIS WIFE DIED.
YOU AND YOUR DUMB SEX JOKES.
FORGIVE ME, HUMOR IS A GREAT ICEBREAKER AND A WAY TO CALM THE JITTERS.
IT'S ALWAYS NERVE-WRACKIN MEETING PEOPL FOR THE FIRST TIME.
EVEN AFTER ALL THIS TIME IN LIFESTYLE TOGETHER?

NEVER GOES AWAY.
WHICH OF THE TWO OF YOU INITIATED THE IDEA OF SWINGING?
THAT WOULD BE ME.
THAT'S GOOD. MOST SUCCESSFUL SWINGER COUPLES ORIGINATED FROM THE WOMAN.
WHY'S THAT?
A LOT OF GUYS ARE ASSHOLES AND DON'T RESPECT BOUNDARIES AS WELL AS WOMEN SEEM TO.
FOR THIS TO WORK, WE ALL MUST RESPECT EACH OTHER'S RELATIONSHIPS.
THAT IS MUSIC TO MY EARS. I'LL DRINK TO THAT.
SO SHE ROPED YOU IN WITH A BUNCH OF THREESOMES? TELL ME ALL ABOUT IT.

HOURS LATER.
WELL, IT'S ABOUT TIME TO CALL IT A NIGHT.
AWW, WE DON'T WANT THE NIGHT TO END.
YOU WANT TO GET A HOTEL ROOM?
THAT SOUNDS LOVELY.
LET ME TEXT MY MOTHER THAT WE'LL BE OUT A BIT LATER, SHE'S WATCHING OUR KIDS.
DONE.
LET'S GO.

AND JUST LIKE THAT, AFTER ALL THE FAILURES, ANNOYING PEOPLE, AND PROBLEMS WE HAD TO OVERCOME GETTING TO THIS MOMENT... WE WERE FINALLY THERE.
I WAS SCARED, BUT EXCITED.
MORE WORRIED ABOUT HOW DAN MIGHT REACT THAN ANYTHING. MR. WORRYWART WHO WAS SO CONCERNED ABOUT GIVING OUT PERSONAL INFORMATION WAS TELLING THEM EVERYTHING ABOUT US.
WE JUST FELT SO COMFORTABLE WITH THEM, LIKE WE WERE OLD FRIENDS.
I'VE BEEN A HIGH SCHOOL TEACHER FOR FOUR YEARS NOW. I'VE ALWAYS WANTED TO BE A WRITER BUT GAVE THAT UP FOR A FEW YEARS AFTER A SEA OF REJECTION LETTERS.
I STARTED A NEW NOVEL RECENTLY SO I'M GOING TO GIVE IT ANOTHER SHOT.
THAT'S FANTASTIC! I'D LOVE TO GIVE IT A READ WHEN YOU FINISH IT. I KNOW A FEW PEOPLE IN THE PUBLISHING BIZ.
ENOUGH WORK TALK, PAY ATTENTION TO ME NOW.
I CAN NEVER SAY NO TO YOU, DARLING.

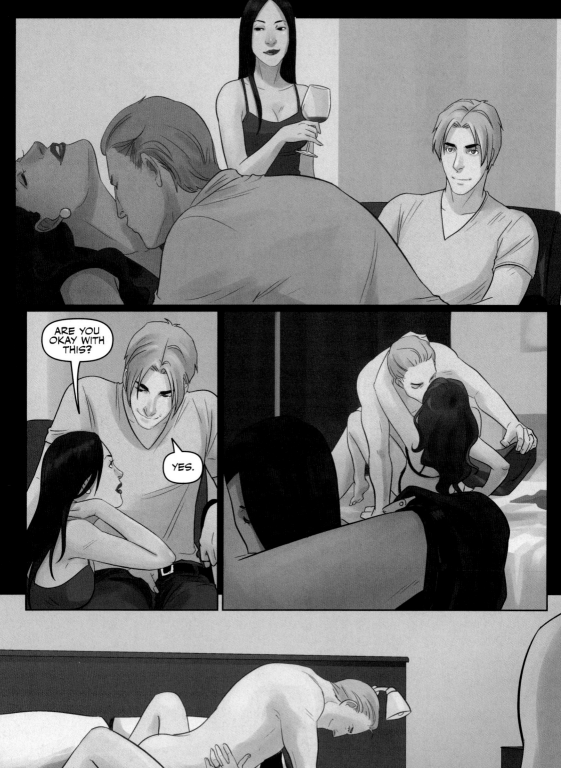

ARE YOU OKAY WITH THIS?

YES.

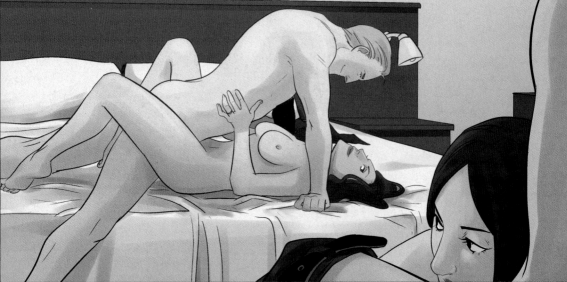

SWAP?

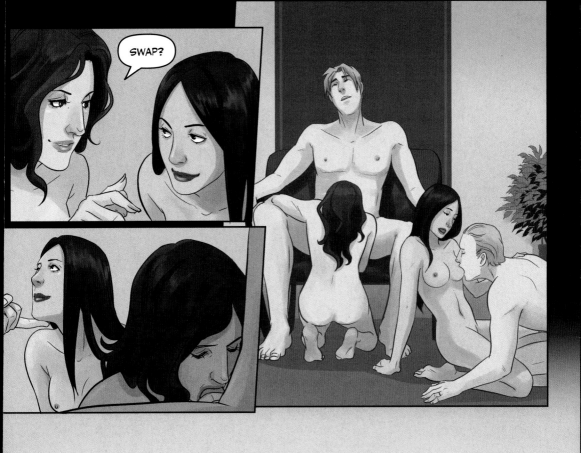

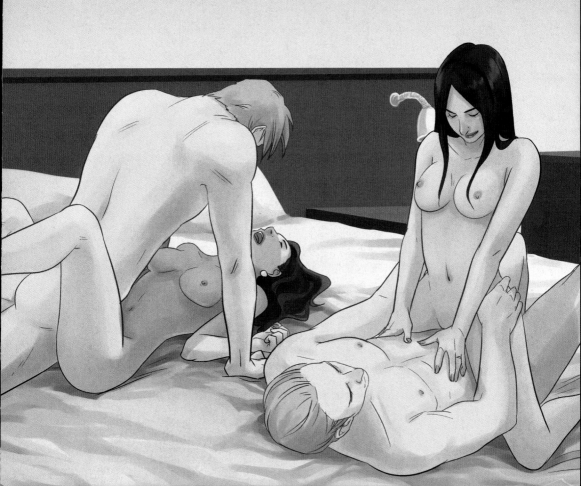

I'D ALMOST GIVEN UP HOPE, BUT THIS WAS EVERYTHING I WANTED IT TO BE.
IT REALLY IS ABOUT FINDING THE RIGHT PEOPLE.

WELL? YOU HAVEN'T SAID MUCH.
I'M STILL IN A STATE OF SHOCK.
THAT WAS AWESOME.
REALLY? OH DAN, THAT MAKES ME SO HAPPY. I WAS SO NERVOUS ABOUT HOW YOU'D REACT.
NO REGRETS?
HA HA, NOPE. WHO'D HAVE THOUGHT I NEEDED TO LIKE THE GUY FOR ME TO BE OKAY WITH HIM BANGING YOU?
BANGING? YOU DRUNK ASS. LET'S GO HOME.
AFTERCARE IS SOMETHING YOU DON'T THINK ABOUT WHEN YOU START THIS KIND OF THING, BUT I READ ABOUT IT ONLINE.
NEVER CAME, BAD BOY. YOU WANT TO TAKE ME HOME AND FINISH ME OFF?
YES, MA'AM.

TURNS OUT AFTER A SWINGING EXPERIENCE, THE BEST THING IS TO BE SUPER AFFECTIONATE AND CONTINUE THE SEX AT HOME SO YOUR PARTNER FEELS LOVED AND LIKE THE MOST IMPORTANT PERSON IN YOUR LIFE.
SHHH, IT'S SO LATE.
CLICK
‹IT'S FOUR AM! WHERE HAVE YOU BEEN?›*
*TRANSLATED FROM MANDARIN.
WE LOST TRACK OF TIME, MOM. SORRY. HOW ARE THE KIDS?
‹YOU NEED TO TALK TO ASHLEY ABOUT BOYS.›
‹SHE'S TOO YOUNG TO BE TEXTING BOYS AT NIGHT.›
‹YOU DON'T WANT HER TO GROW UP TO BE A SLUT.›
I WILL, AND THANKS SO MUCH FOR WATCHING THEM. NIGHT.
WHAT'D SHE SAY?
SHE WAS RAMBLING ON ABOUT SOMETHING.

SOME COUPLES VIEW SWINGING PURELY AS FOREPLAY.
YOU KNOW HOW SHE IS.
THAT WORKS FOR ME.
HEY, STUD, YOU GOT SOMETHING FOR ME?

12:20 PM, SATURDAY.
ARE YOU GOING TO SLEEP ALL DAY? WE HAD TO MAKE OUR OWN BREAKFAST, BUT LUNCH TOO IS NOT COOL.
HEY, KIDDOS, SORRY WE WERE OUT LATE LAST NIGHT.
CAN WE GO TO THE PARK?
SURE.
YOU PROMISED YOU'D FIX MY BIKE TODAY.
DON'T LET DAD DO IT, YOU KNOW HE'S TERRIBLE AT FIXING THINGS.
I WON'T DO IT, BLAKE, MOMMY WILL. DADDY HAS A TUTOR SESSION THIS AFTERNOON ANYWAY.

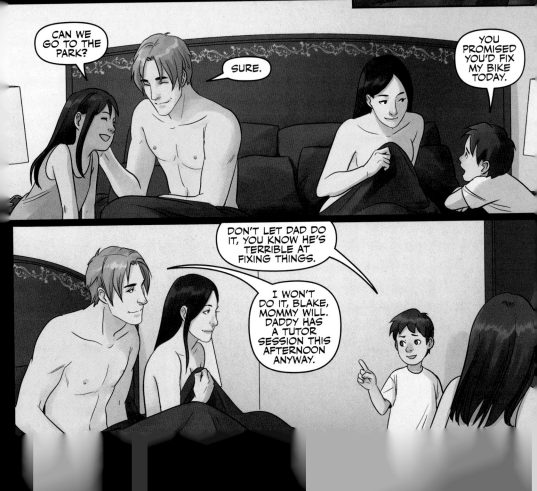

WELL, IT'S THE MORNING AFTER.
ANY HUNGOVER THOUGHTS?
NO, I WAS WORRIED I'D BE FILLED WITH REGRET, BUT I'M FINE.
GOOD, BECAUSE WE GOT AN INVITE TO A SANCTORUM PARTY TONIGHT IN BEVERLY HILLS.
THAT'S THE *EYES WIDE SHUT* KIND OF THING WITH THE MASKS?
YEAH, AND I KNOW WE TALKED ABOUT ONLY DOING LIFESTYLE LIKE MAYBE ONCE A MONTH, BUT GETTING ON THE GUEST LIST IS HARD.
THE MEMBERSHIP FEE IF WE WANT TO JOIN IS LIKE TEN THOUSAND A YEAR. WHICH IS RIDICULOUS...
...BUT WE CAN GO CHECK IT OUT FOR FREE.

ANOTHER THING I FOUND IN MY READING UP ON LIFESTYLE IS THAT NEW COUPLES TEND TO GO A LITTLE WILD AT FIRST, UNTIL THEY FIND THEIR BALANCE.
IT'S NOT UNCOMMON FOR COUPLES TO HAVE MULTIPLE ENCOUNTERS IN THEIR FIRST FEW WEEKS ONCE ACTIVE.
PART OF THE FUN IS FIGURING OUT WHAT WORKS FOR YOU AND HOW OFTEN.
CHAMPAGNE?
THANK YOU.
I'M SO HAPPY THIS SEEMS TO BE WORKING OUT FOR US.
THIS PLACE IS AMAZING.

CATHY HAS DONE HER HOMEWORK ON HOW TO HANDLE ME IN THESE SITUATIONS.
WE'RE ALWAYS IN PHYSICAL CONTACT AND SHE NEVER LEAVES ME ALONE.
NICE TO MEET YOU.
SHE ASKS ME AT EVERY STEP IF I'M OKAY WITH WHAT'S HAPPENING.
I'M NOT QUITE AS GUNG HO ABOUT IT ALL AS SHE IS, BUT WE'RE ALL CONSENTING ADULTS AND NO ONE IS GETTING HURT...SO WHY NOT?

YOU WANT TO TRY AND JOIN IN?
SURE, I NEED TO PEE FIRST, THOUGH.
BATHROOM'S THERE.
I'LL BE HERE.
HI THERE, I'M JEFF. WHAT'S YOUR NAME?
CATHY.
ARE YOU HERE ALONE?
NO, I'M HERE WITH MY HUSBAND. HE'S IN THE RESTROOM.

MY WIFE IS ROAMING AROUND SOMEWHERE. WE'RE HAVING A PARTY NEXT MONTH, PERHAPS YOU TWO WOULD LIKE TO COME?
I'D HAVE TO MAKE SURE IT'S OKAY WITH MY HUSBAND, BUT MAYBE.
CAN YOU GIVE ME AN EMAIL I CAN SEND THE INVITE TO?
WE USE A JOINT ONE, DRINKSINLA@ GMAIL.COM.
UH... WHAT'S GOING ON HERE?
THIS IS JEFF, HE'S INVITING US TO A PARTY.
PLEASURE TO MEET YOU, WHAT'S YOUR NAME?
LEAVING.
WHAT THE FUCK? THAT WAS RUDE.

I LEAVE YOU ALONE FOR ONE SECOND AND YOU'RE FLIRTING WITH SOME SINGLE GUY?
WHAT?!
I WAS NOT FLIRTING AND HE WAS THERE WITH HIS WIFE.
I GAVE HIM OUR JOINT DRINKSINLA EMAIL ADDRESS. THE ADDRESS YOU SET UP.
YOU TALK TO THESE PEOPLE ONLINE FOR HOURS AT A TIME; I CHAT WITH ONE GUY FOR ONE MINUTE AND YOU FREAK THE FUCK OUT.
I'M SORRY. I PANICK WHEN I CAME OUT A SAW YOU TALKING TO I GOT REALLY JEALO AND ANGRY.

WHAT DO YOU WANT TO DO TONIGHT? MY MOM IS TAKING THE KIDS TO SEE A MOVIE AND THEY'RE SLEEPING OVER AT HER PLACE.
A COUPLE I WAS TALKING TO IS GOING TO LIFESTYLE CLUB TONIGHT AND WANTS US TO MEET THEM THERE.
I DON'T KNOW, I'M STILL NOT HAPPY ABOUT WHAT HAPPENED AT THAT PARTY.
I SAID I WAS SORRY FOR THAT.
THAT WAS SO EMBARRASSING.
AND YOU ACCUSED ME OF FLIRTING. I DIDN'T DO ANYTHING WRONG.
I KNOW. I WAS WRONG AND I'M SORRY. YOU'RE SO BEAUTIFUL AND MEAN SO MUCH TO ME...
...MY PRIMAL INSTINCTS KICKED IN.

WHATEVER.
I'M YOURS, YOU KNOW, AND I WAS FOLLOWING ALL YOUR RULES.
YES.
YOU **ARE** MINE.

LET'S JUST GO. WE CAN MAKE NEW FRIENDS, WE DON'T HAVE TO DO ANYTHING.
STOP TALKING.

Lifestyle Club
IDS PLEASE.
IS THERE A WAY TO CHECK IF A COUPLE WE'RE MEETING IS HERE YET?
SHEILA!
I SWEAR TO GOD, CARL. IF YOU DON'T STOP YELLING AND USE THE GOD DAMN WALKIE TALKIES, I'M GOING TO TIE YOU UP AND JAM MY RABBIT* UP YOUR ASS UNTIL YOU CAN'T SIT FOR A WEEK.
*A TYPE OF VIBRATOR.
UH, HI, WE JUST WANTED TO KNOW IF JOHN AND CAROL WESTLAKE ARE HERE YET? WE'RE SUPPOSED TO MEET THEM.

I KNOW THEM AND YES, THEY ARE. NICE COUPLE.
RIGHT THERE.
HI.
HEYA, THANKS FOR COMING.
WE'VE ENJOYED CHATTING WITH YOU THIS PAST MONTH.
UH... YEAH.

WE'RE LOOKING FORWARD TO GETTING TO KNOW YOU A BIT BETTER, DAN. TALKING TO CATHY ONLINE, WE REALLY FEEL LIKE WE'VE GOTTEN TO KNOW HER.
UH, YEAH...ABOUT THAT...COME HERE... I NEED TO CONFESS SOMETHING.
THAT'S N PRETENDING TO BE ME, HE OES THAT TO GET RID OF AGGRESSIVE GUYS.
ARE YOU KIDDING ME? THAT'S HILARIOUS.
HA HA HA HA
WHAT'S SO FUNNY?
OH, NOTHING... JUST GIRL TALK.

CATHY TOLD ME YOU'RE A LAWYER. WHAT KIND?
TRADEMARK AND COPYRIGHT.
CAN WE GET THE BOTTLE OF KRUG I BROUGHT? WE'RE GOING TO MOVE TO A TABLE.
HERE'S TO US AND THOSE THAT WANT TO BE LIKE US.
I'LL DRINK TO THAT.
I'M GLAD WE BROUGHT THE GOOD BOTTLE. THIS IS SMOOTH.
YEAH... I LIKE IT, I DON'T NORMALLY DRINK CHAMPAGNE.
AWW, YOU'RE AN ADORABLE DRUNK.

SHOULD WE TAKE THIS TO A PLAYROOM?
NEXT TIME. WE GOT INTO A BIG FIGHT RECENTLY; I DON'T THINK DAN WOULD BE INTO IT TONIGHT.
HE SEEMS FINE.
LET'S FIND A SPOT.

WE'LL TAKE THE COUCH. YOU TWO TAKE THE CHAIR.
THAT WORKS.
ARE YOU OKAY WITH THIS?
OF COURSE HE IS.

YOU'RE NOT HARD.
LET ME GO DOWN ON YOU.
YOUR TURN.
ARE YOU OKAY? YOU'RE STILL NOT HARD.

JUST GIVE US A MINUTE, WE'LL BE RIGHT BACK.
WHAT'S GOING ON?
THIS HAS NEVER HAPPENED TO ME BEFORE.
I CAN'T GET HARD.
LET ME HELP.
I DON'T THINK IT'S GOING TO HAPPEN, HONEY. I'M SORRY.
YOU HAD A LOT TO DRINK AND IT'S NOT A BIG DEAL.
I DON'T WANT TO LET YOU DOWN.
ARE YOU MAD?
OF COURSE NOT. I LOVE YOU. LET'S JUST GO HOME.

WE'RE GOING TO CALL IT A NIGHT. THANKS FOR THE LOVELY EVENING.
HEY, DAN, MEET ME IN THE MEN'S LOCKER ROOM. I HAVE SOMETHING FOR YOU.
MAYBE LIFESTYLE ISN'T FOR US.
I DON'T WANT TO QUIT.
I LOVE YOU, DUMB ASS, BUT I'M NOT SURE YOU MEAN THAT. DON'T JUST TELL ME WHAT I WANT TO HEAR.
I'M NOT MAD OR EVEN UPSET, BUT IF YOU CAN'T GET HARD MAYBE THAT'S YOUR MIND TELLING YOU NOT TO DO THIS STUFF.
JOHN GAVE ME SOME VIAGRA.
HE SAID THE SAME THING HAPPENS TO HIM SOMETIMES AND HE HAS THESE JUST IN CASE.
CAN YOU TRY ONE WHEN WE GET HOME?

WE'RE HOME! DID YOU MISS US?
<IS HE ALWAYS LIKE THAT IN THE MORNING?>
LET'S GO BACK DOWNSTAIRS, KIDS.
CHECK YOUR PHONE.
Meet me in the bathroom with that thing, I might let you slip it in the back door.

THIS IS THE FIFTH WEEK IN A ROW WE'VE TRIED THIS RAID. MULTIPLE FAILS, THIS IS THE FARTHEST WE'VE GOTTEN.
THIS ROOM IS A CHESS BOARD. I'VE READ ABOUT IT ONLINE, BUT TO THWART PEOPLE LEARNING HOW TO DO IT FROM SPOILER SITES, THEY HAVE SOME RANDOM ELEMENTS.
THIS ONLINE DATING STUFF IS A BIT INSANE. SHE MISSED OUT ON IT ENTIRELY, BUT I BARELY DID ANY OF IT EITHER.
PRETENDING TO BE CATHY IS BOTH FUN AND FRUSTRATING.
ABOUT HALF OF THE DUDES I CHAT WITH ARE KIND OF ASSHOLES ABOUT IT. CATHY THINKS I'M OVERCRITICAL ABOUT IT, BUT I AM CHOOSING TO BE PICKY.
CHAT
FUN_COUPLE
Hey, this is Cathy my husband's name is Dan.
OKAY, EVERYONE BACK?
DAN, CAN YOU MOVE UP TWO AND OVER ONE WITHOUT TOUCHING THE OTHER SQUARES?
LIKE THE HORSE?
YESSIR.
DONE.

I NEED TO PEE. LET'S TAKE A QUICK BIO BREAK BEFORE WE START THE NEXT PART?
SOUNDS GOOD. LET'S TAKE FIVE. DAN, DON'T STEP OFF THAT SQUARE.

CHAT

● FUN_COUPLE

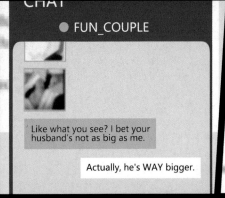

Like what you see? I bet your husband's not as big as me.

Actually, he's WAY bigger.

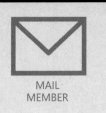

MAIL
MEMBER

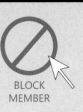

BLOCK
MEMBER

CHAT

CHAT

● SWINGFLY

Your profile has no pics, can you share some?

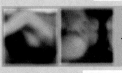 +2

I meant face pics, we don't want nudes.

We don't share face pics we don't want people to know we do this.

Well then how am I supposed to know what you look like?

When we meet.

My husband's not going to meet you if you don't share some simple face/body pics ...clothed.

SWINGFLY HAS BLOCKED YOU.

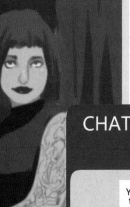

Hello Kasidie, We are your hosts @The exclusive Lifestyle Playground and the

Check out our community page here

CHAT

● WENDY

You're the first unicorn I've talked to through this site, how do you like it?

I love it. I'm into Haematophilia, do you know what that is?

Nope, new one for me.

I like to have sex while we lightly cut each other with a small razor.

That's a new one on me but we're going to pass. Good luck with it.

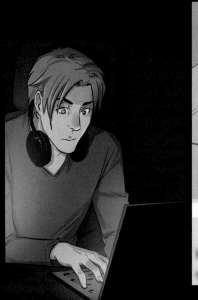

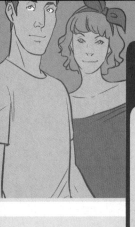

CHAT

● ROCKABILLY69

I hope you're sane, I've had some crazy chats on here.

We're pretty old school normal. I get the same. My name's Dave, my wife is Colette.

There are guys on here pretending to be women, you know. Most of them just trying to collect nude pics of people. It's why we don't share nudes.

AND WHO SAYS MEN CAN'T MULTITASK?
Ready Check
YES
NO
CAN I GET A SNACK?
IT'S A LITTLE LATE FOR A SNACK, ISN'T IT?
MUTE
PLEASE, DADDY?
THERE ARE SOME OTTER POPS IN THE FREEZER, BUT DON'T TELL YOUR MOM.
UNMUTE

OKAY, EVERYONE SAID THEY WERE READY, LET'S DO THIS. FOCUS, EVERYONE!
YEAH, LET'S DO THIS.
OKAY, DAN, PLACE THE GEMS IN HIS EYES.
DAN?

DAN, DO IT NOW!

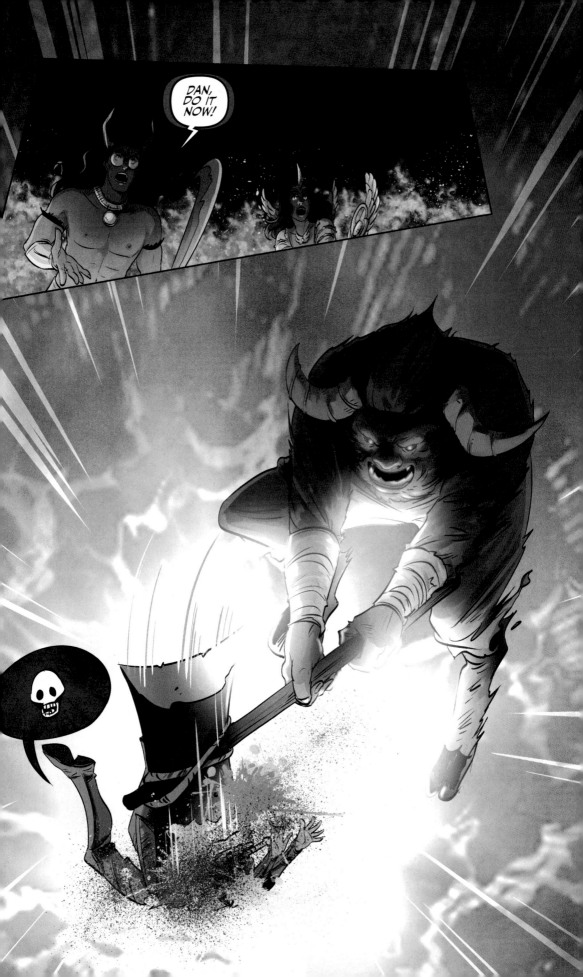

OOOOSH

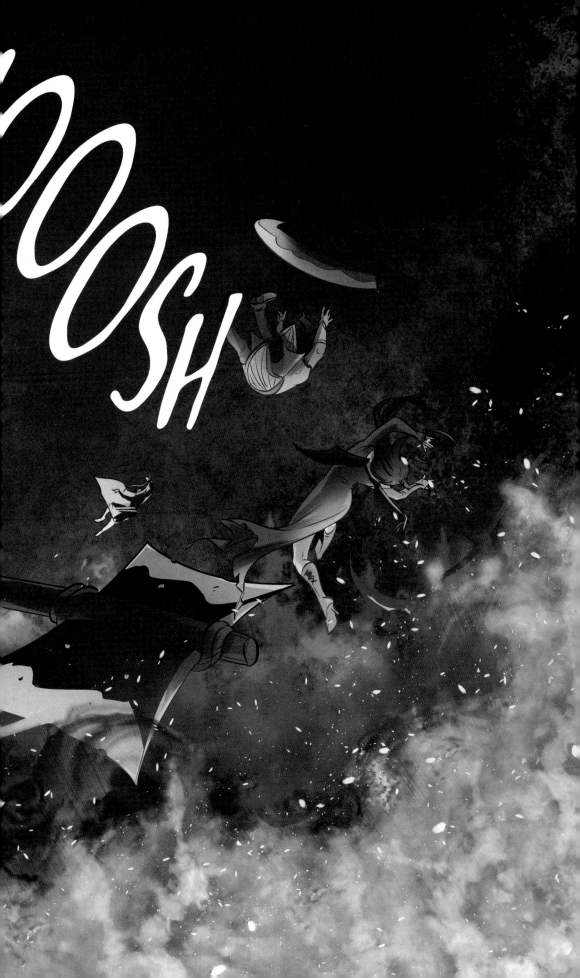

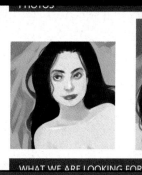
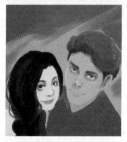
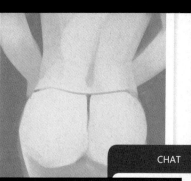

CHAT

WHAT WE ARE LOOKING FOR

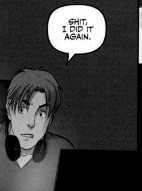

SHIT, I DID IT AGAIN.

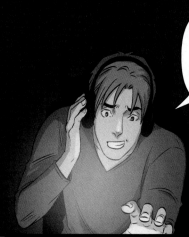

GUYS, SORRY THIS WIFI IS *SO* BAD. I'VE RUN SPEED TESTS AND WE'RE GETTING LESS THAN HALF OF WHAT WE'RE PAYING FOR.

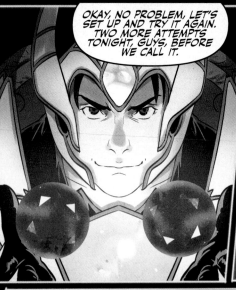

OKAY, NO PROBLEM, LET'S SET UP AND TRY IT AGAIN. TWO MORE ATTEMPTS TONIGHT, GUYS, BEFORE WE CALL IT.

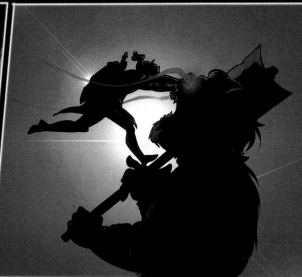

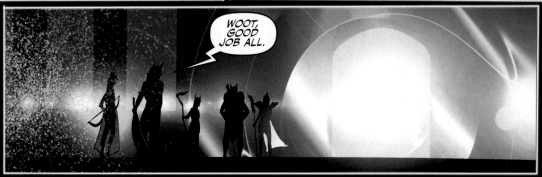

WOOT, GOOD JOB ALL.

OKAY, WE'VE GOT THIRTY SECONDS TO GET THROUGH THAT DOOR BEFORE THE ROOM GETS HIT WITH FIREBALLS.
DID YOU SAY ASHLEY COULD HAVE AN OTTER POP?
UH... YEAH.
IT'S BEDTIME, THIS MUCH SUGAR WILL JUST KEEP HER AWAKE.
WE AGREED NO SWEETS BEFORE BED. SHE'S GOING TO BE UP FOR A WHILE NOW. YOU DEAL WITH HER.
I THOUGHT WE AGREED YOU WOULDN'T TELL MOM?
SHE CAUGHT ME WITH IT, AND SHE'S SCARY WHEN SHE'S MAD.
TELL ME ABOUT IT. GO UP TO YOUR ROOM -- I'LL COME READ YOU A BOOK IN A FEW.

MONTHS LATER.
MY DAILY ROUTINE IS PRETTY MUCH THE SAME, BUT I'M HAPPIER NOW.
WE'VE HAD A FEW MORE SUCCESSFUL ENCOUNTERS AND DAN HAS BECOME A VIAGRA FIEND.
WE NEED AN OVERALL DEAL. IT WOULD GENERATE LESS MONEY PER TRAILER WITH THE STUDIO, BUT IT WOULD GUARANTEE US TEN TIMES THE REVENUE.
DO WE HAVE ENOUGH PEOPLE TO PULL THAT OFF?
NO, BUT ONE OF THE FREELANCE GROUPS IS WILLING TO DROP THEIR COST IF WE GUARANTEE THEM MORE WORK, WHICH, WITH THIS DEAL WE CAN DO.
IF YOU CAN GET THE STUDIO DEAL YOU HAVE OUR APPROVAL.
I'LL SET A MEETING AND PITCH THEIR WHOLE TEAM.
AS A COUPLE WE'RE MORE AFFECTIONATE THAN EVER.
WE HAVE REGULAR DATE NIGHTS FOR JUST THE TWO OF US.

HAS IMPROVED MARKEDLY.
IT SEEMS ODD THAT OUR HAVING SEX WITH OTHER PEOPLE WOULD BRING US CLOSER TOGETHER... BUT IT HAS.
DAN HAS SURPRISED ME WITH ROMANTIC SCAVENGER HUNTS.
HE'S BEEN SENDING ME FLOWERS AT WORK, WHICH HE NEVER USED TO DO.
ARE YOU DONE FOR THE DAY?
YEAH, BUT DAN TEXTED ME HE LEFT SOMETHING FOR ME. CAN YOU GO CHECK?

THIS WAS LEFT AT THE FRONT DESK AND THERE'S A CAR SERVICE WAITING FOR YOU OUT FRONT.
THANKS, CHRIS, YOU CAN TAKE OFF FOR THE NIGHT. I'LL SEE YOU MONDAY.
HAVE A GREAT WEEKEND.
YOU TOO.
A SURPRISE NIGHT OUT.

RIGHT THIS WAY, MADAM.
HEY, BEAUTIFUL.
WHAT'S THE OCCASION? DID I FORGET OUR ANNIVERSARY OR SOMETHING?
NOT AT ALL. IT'S JUST A REGULAR FRIDAY, BUT I WANTED TO TREAT YOU TO A SPECIAL NIGHT OUT.

THE VIEW FROM UP HERE ALMOST MAKES YOU FORGET ABOUT SKID ROW A FEW BLOCKS AWAY.
CAN YOU BELIEVE NEXT YEAR WILL BE OUR TENTH WEDDING ANNIVERSARY?
MARRYING YOU WAS THE BEST DECISION I EVER MADE.
I'M LUCKY TO HAVE YOU.
EVERY MORNING I WAKE UP NEXT TO YOU IS A GIFT.
AWW, THAT'S SWEET. I REALLY CAN'T IMAGINE MY LIFE WITHOUT YOU.
I KNOW THIS LIFESTYLE STUFF HASN'T ALWAYS BEEN EASY FOR YOU, BUT IT SEEMS TO BE WORKING FOR US.

HOURS LATER.
SO WHAT'S ON TAP FOR THE REST OF THE NIGHT, LOVERBOY? YOU GET A ROOM HERE?
YES, AND THERE'S A CLUB HERE TOO. THOUGHT IT MIGHT BE FUN TO VISIT A VANILLA* ONE.
*NON-LIFESTYLE CLUB.

THMMPTHMMPTHMPTHMMPTHMMPTHMMPTHMPTHMMPTHMMP
ARE YOU HAVING A GOOD TIME?
WHAT?!
I CAN'T HEAR YOU! IT'S SO LOUD!
LET'S GRAB ANOTHER DRINK.
HEY, SEXY.
YOU WANNA DANCE?

THAT'S MY WIFE, FRIEND. I'D APPRECIATE IT IF YOU DIDN'T PUT YOUR HANDS ON HER AGAIN.
MY HERO.
LET'S CALL IT A NIGHT.

NO MAN HAS EVER TOUCHED ME AT A LIFESTYLE CLUB WITHOUT ASKING FIRST.
I'VE NEVER FELT PRESSURED INTO ANYTHING.
THE RESPECT FOR RELATIONSHIPS AND THE CONSENT NECESSARY IS RADICALLY DIFFERENT THAN WHAT HAPPENS IN THE REAL WORLD.
IT'S THE EXACT OPPOSITE OF WHAT PEOPLE EXPECT.

THE LAST COUPLE MONTHS HAVE BEEN THE MOST PEACEFUL AND AMAZING TIME OF MY LIFE.
I NEVER IN A MILLION YEARS THOUGHT OUR HAVING SEX WITH OTHER PEOPLE WOULD MAKE OUR RELATIONSHIP BETTER... BUT IT HAS.
ANYONE KNOW HOW OLD ROMEO AND JULIET WERE AT THE TIME OF THIS STORY?
HANNAH?
JULIET WAS THIRTEEN, BUT WE DON'T KNOW HOW OLD ROMEO WAS. IT'S ASSUMED HE WAS OLDER.
THAT'S EXACTLY RIGHT, HANNAH, I'M IMPRESSED.
BRRNNNGGG
I HAD SOME QUESTIONS. ARE YOU AVAILABLE AFTER SCHOOL AT ALL?
I'M HERE FOR A HALF HOUR AFTER SIXTH EVERY DAY, DROP BY ANY TIME.

I'M STILL A BIT MORE HESITANT AND RESERVED THAN CATHY IS ABOUT LETTING SOME OF OUR LIFESTYLE FRIENDS INTO OUR REAL LIFE.
I LIKE THE SEPARATION. IT'S LIKE I HAVE A SECRET LIFE, AND DAN THE SCHOOLTEACHER IS MY SECRET IDENTITY.
HI, MR. LINCOLN.
IS NOW A BAD TIME?
NO, IT'S FINE, YOU HAD SOME SHAKESPEARE QUESTIONS?
NO, I WANTED TO TALK TO YOU ABOUT SOMETHING ELSE.

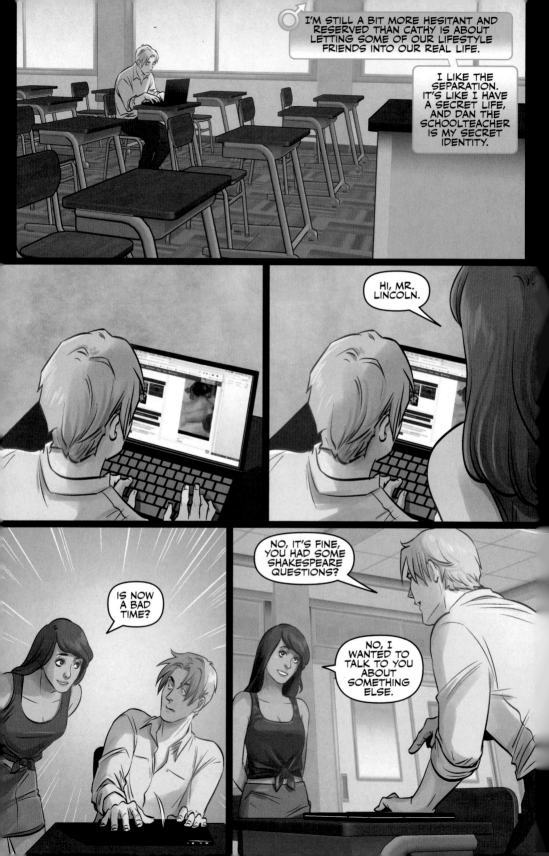

WHAT CAN I DO FOR YOU?
I...UH...I'M SO SORRY, BUT CAN I HAVE YOUR AUTOGRAPH? I LOVE THIS PIECE YOU WROTE.
LITERATURE
The End of Innocence
by Dan Lincoln
OH MY GOD, I CAN'T BELIEVE YOU EVEN FOUND THIS.
I WROTE THIS TEN YEARS AGO. IT'S THE ONLY THING I'VE EVER HAD PUBLISHED.
LITERATURE
I LOVED IT.
I DON'T THINK MY WIFE HAS EVER READ THIS.
WELL, THAT'S HER FAULT.
DON'T DO THAT.

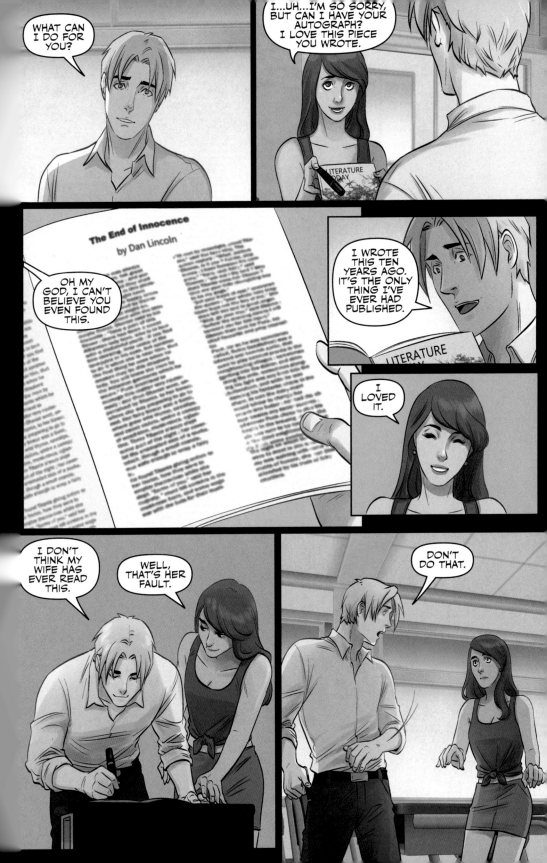

HANNAH, YOU'RE A BEAUTIFUL YOUNG GIRL, BUT I'M TWICE YOUR AGE AND THIS IS HIGHLY INAPPROPRIATE. I'M SORRY IF I SOMEHOW MADE YOU THINK DIFFERENTLY.
I JUST LOVE LISTENING TO YOU TALK ABOUT THESE WRITERS AND BOOKS. YOU'RE SO PASSIONATE.
IT'S OKAY, I'M NOT GOING TO REPORT YOU OR ANYTHING, BUT I'M A MARRIED MAN WITH A FAMILY AND I LOVE MY WIFE.
YOU NEED TO WRITE MORE. YOUR STORY REALLY SPOKE TO ME. YOU HAVE A GIFT.
THAT MEANS A LOT, THANK YOU. I'M WORKING ON A NEW NOVEL, MAYBE YOU CAN READ IT BEFORE I SEND IT OUT FOR SUBMISSION AND LET ME KNOW WHAT YOU THINK.

PULLING OUT THESE OLD REJECTION LETTERS KIND OF STINGS.
Mr. Dan Lincoln
e appreciate your submission
but this doesn't meet our current
requirements.
cerely yours
I SHOULD FRAME ALL THESE IF I EVER GET PUBLISHED FOR REAL.
I'M HAPPIER IN MY PERSONAL LIFE THAN EVER, BUT I WANT TO BE A REAL WRITER MORE THAN ANYTHING.

NOT ALL THAT NERVOUS.
CONFIDENCE HAS NEVER BEEN A PROBLEM FOR ME.
I KNOW PEOPLE ARE TRICKLING IN, BUT LET'S GET STARTED, SHALL WE?
I'M CATHY CHANG, MANY OF YOU KNOW ME ALREADY. FOR THE PAST FIVE YEARS WE'VE DONE A SERIES OF TRAILERS FOR YOUR FILMS.
SINCE YOU'RE IN THE FILM BUSINESS, I THOUGHT IT APPROPRIATE MY TEAM PUT TOGETHER A SHORT FILM TO SHOW WHAT I'M PITCHING, RATHER THAN JUST TALKING AT YOU.
HERE WE GO.
IN MANY WAYS, THE

STATISTICS POINT TO THE TRAILER ITSELF HAVING THE GREATEST IMPACT ON PEOPLE'S DECISION TO SEE A FILM ON OPENING WEEKEND.
SHORT BUT SWEET, JUST LIKE A REAL MOVIE TRAILER.
QUESTION.
WILL YOU BE OUR POINT OF CONTACT FOR EVERYTHING GOING FORWARD IF WE AGREE TO THIS OVERALL DEAL YOU'RE PITCHING?
YES, I WILL BE THE LIAISON BETWEEN THE STUDIO AND MY TEAM. ANY PROBLEMS OR QUESTIONS YOU MIGHT HAVE, I'LL EITHER ANSWER OR FIND THE ANSWER FOR YOU.
WELL, THAT'S FANTASTIC, I'M SOLD. YOU'VE DONE SUCH GREAT WORK FOR US IN THE PAST.

I APPRECIATE THE VOTE OF CONFIDENCE. ANY OTHER DEPARTMENTS HAVE ANY QUESTIONS OR CONCERNS I CAN ANSWER OR COMMENT ON?
AND THAT'S ALL WE HAVE, THEN. THANK YOU FOR COMING AND VIEWING OUR PRESENTATION.
CATHY, IS IT?
YES.

WHAT ARE YOU DOING NOW? I HAVE A ROOM AT THE CHATEAU MARMONT. WE COULD GET SOME FOOD AND HAVE SOME DRINKS AND TALK ABOUT HOW WE CAN MAXIMIZE OUR RELATIONSHIP.
I'M MARRIED, I CAN'T DO THAT.
I'M MARRIED, TOO. THAT DOESN'T MEAN WE CAN'T HAVE SOME FUN ON THE SIDE. WHAT PEOPLE DON'T KNOW CAN'T HURT THEM. IT'LL BE GOOD FOR YOUR CAREER.
HARVEY, LET'S NOT GET INTO ANOTHER LEGAL PROBLEM. YOUR LAST ASSISTANT IS STILL PRESSING CHARGES.
SORRY ABOUT THAT.

THANKS, I DIDN'T KNOW WHAT TO DO THERE. I KNOW HE HAS SIGN-OFF ON THIS DEAL.
HE'S A DICKHEAD AND WON'T BE AROUND MUCH LONGER. THIS #METOO MOVEMENT WILL CLAIM HIM, AND RIGHTLY SO.
IT'S GOOD TO SEE YOU.
I LOOK FORWARD TO OUR NEXT PLAY DATE.

NEED TO TELL DAN I RAN INTO CLINT. WE AGREED TO THAT AND IT'S THE RIGHT THING TO DO.
HEY, BABE. HOW WAS YOUR PRESENTATION?
IT WENT WELL. I THINK WE'LL GET IT.
THAT'S FANTASTIC, CONGRATS! I'VE BEEN RESEARCHING SUBMISSION REQUIREMENTS AT ALL THE PUBLISHERS. I SHOULD BE DONE WITH THIS BOOK IN A FEW MONTHS AND WANT TO BE READY.
THAT'S EXCITING. KIDS OKAY?

LIFESTYLE BLEEDING INTO OUR REAL LIVES WAS DAN'S BIGGEST CONCERN, BUT THINGS ARE GOING SO WELL...I DON'T WANT TO CREATE AN UNNECESSARY PROBLEM.
MAYBE I CAN ASK CLINT TO NOT MENTION IT?
THIS GIRL IN MY CLASS HIT ON ME TODAY.
SHE HAD THAT PIECE I PUBLISHED IN COLLEGE AND WANTED ME TO SIGN IT.
GUESS I STILL GOT IT.
OF COURSE YOU DO, HONEY. YOU LOOK GREAT.
IT MOTIVATED ME TO REALLY GET MY SHIT TOGETHER AND TRY AND GET PUBLISHED FOR REAL.
THAT'S GREAT. I'M SORRY, HONEY, BUT I'M SO TIRED I JUST WANT TO SLEEP.

TO BE CONTINUED!

Pegging Wonderland
Written by Matt Hawkins
Art by Linda Sejic
ZZZZZNNGGXX
zzZZZnnXX
MY SWORD... WHY?

BWAHAHA HAHA!

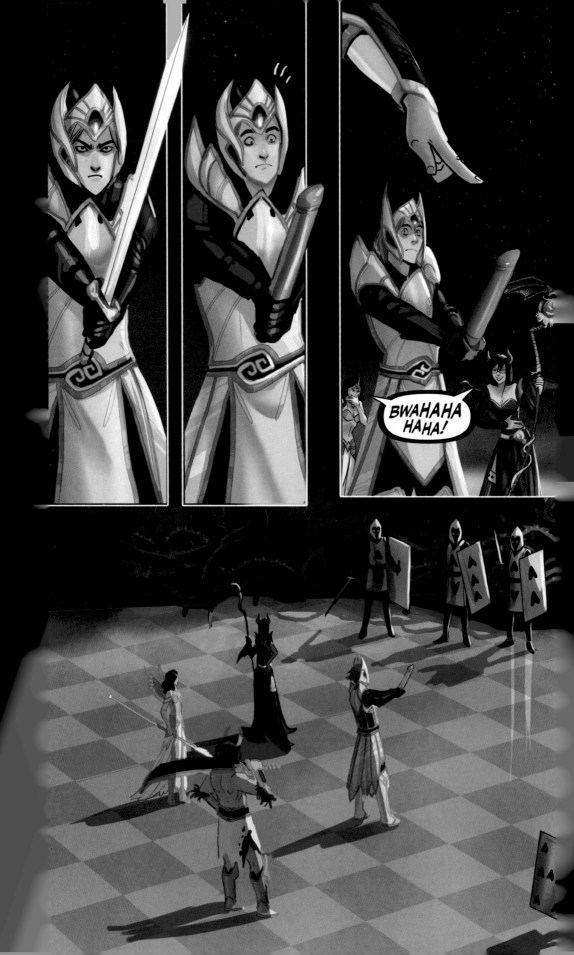

MY, MY.
WHAT DO WE HAVE HERE?

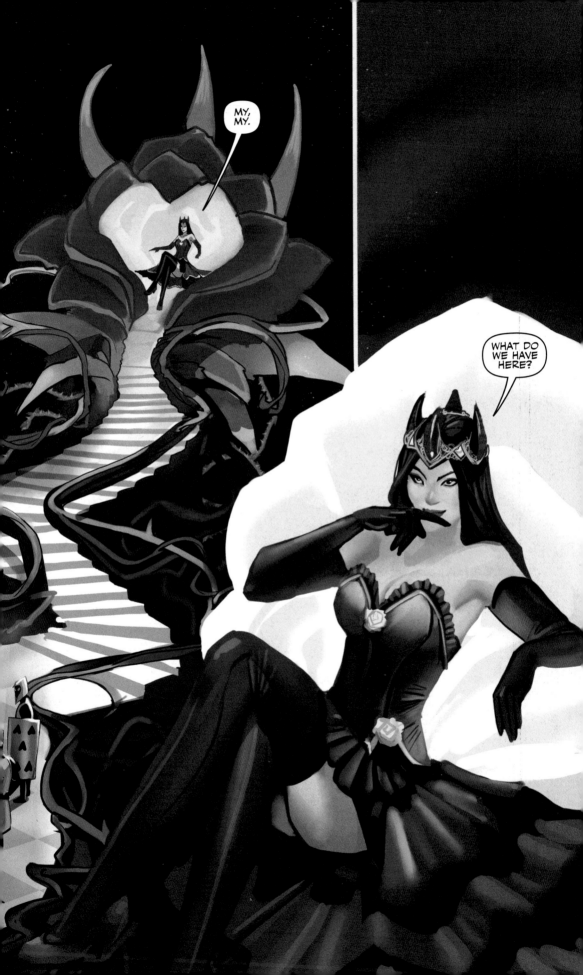

BRING THAT INSTRUMENT OVER HERE FOR MY PLEASURE.
SOUNDS GOOD TO ME.
DON'T! SHE'LL KILL YOU IF YOU DON'T PROPERLY PLEASE HER.
IS THAT TRUE?
YES, IF YOU FAIL TO PLEASE ME IT WILL BE *OFF WITH YOUR HEAD!*
I'LL START WITH THE LITTLE ONE FIRST.

DAN, RUN!
THIS WAY.
DEAD END.
WE'RE LATE.
FOLLOW ME.

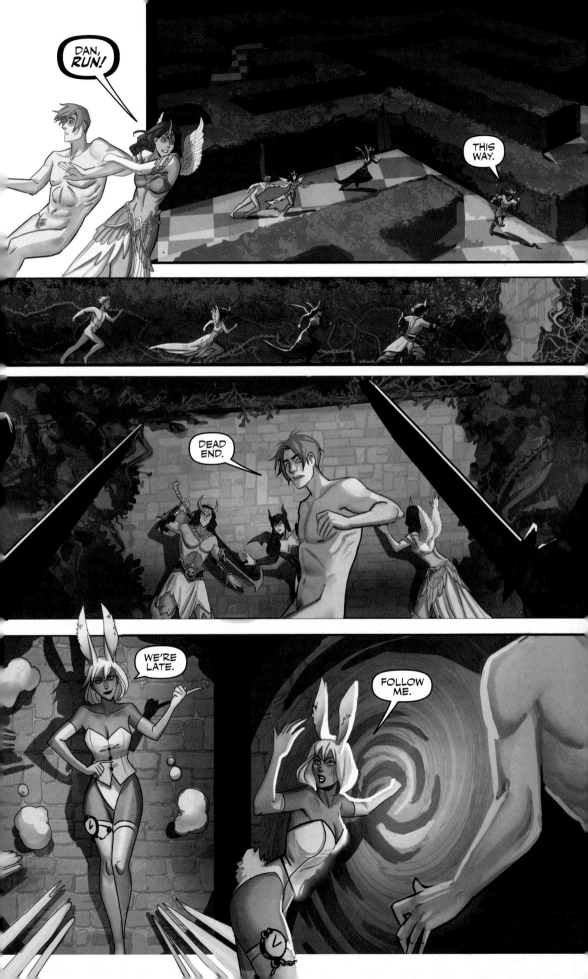

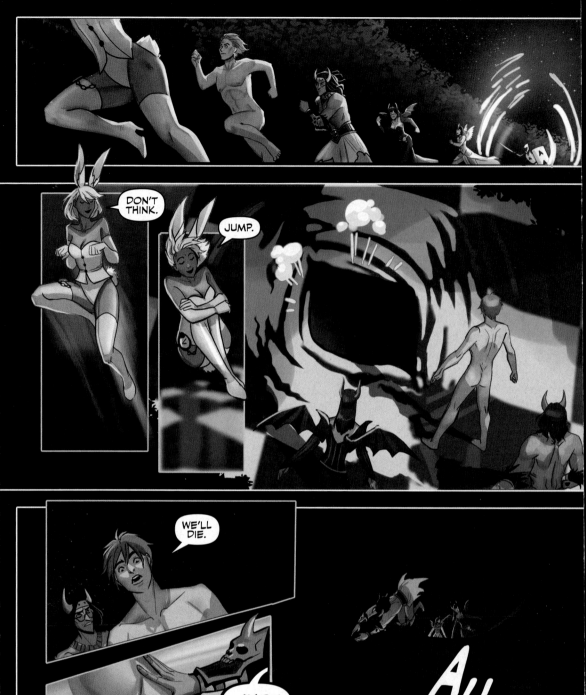

DON'T THINK.

JUMP.

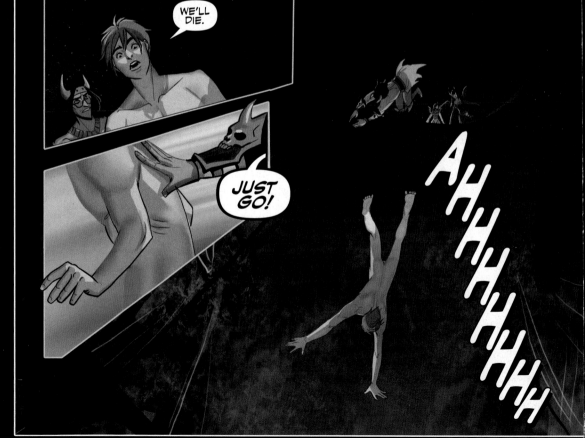

WE'LL DIE.

JUST GO!

AHHHHHHH

THERE YOU ARE.
RIGHT WHERE I WANT YOU.

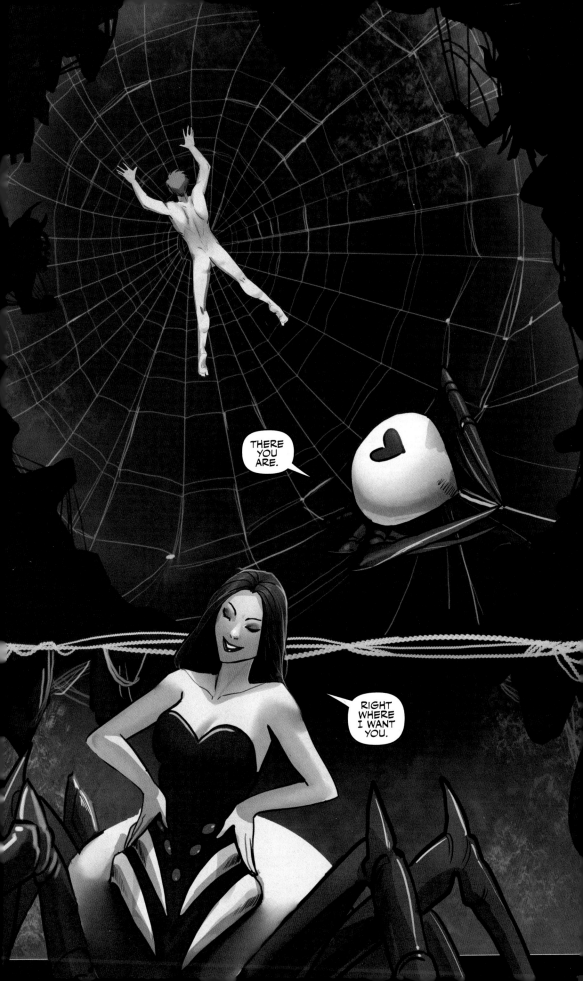

PLEASE, DON'T KILL ME.
I WON'T KILL YOU.
YOU'RE GOING TO LIKE THIS.
AHH?!
MMMM.

AHHHH!
WHAT'S WRONG?
NIGHTMARE.
pegging
END

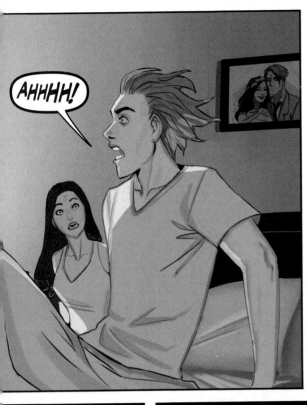

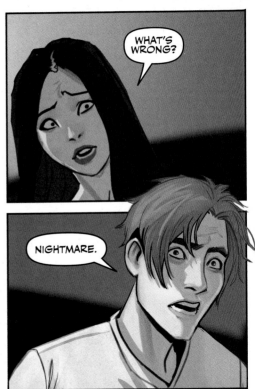

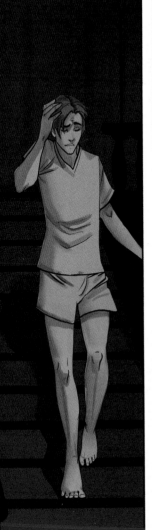

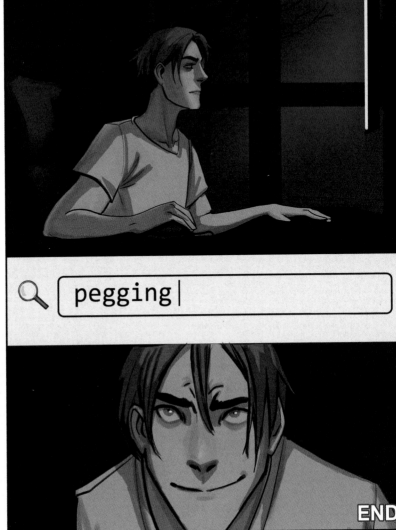

SW

VOLUME

20

MATT HAWKINS

NG

THREE

20

LINDA SEJIC

YISHAN LI

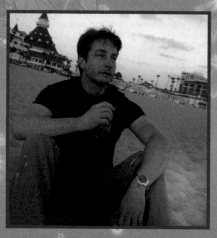

MATT HAWKINS

is a veteran of the initial Image Comics launch. Matt started his career in comic book publishing in 1993 and has been working with Image as a creator, writer, and executive for over twenty years. President/COO of Top Cow since 1998, Matt has created and written over thirty new franchises for Top Cow and Image including THINK TANK, THE TITHE, STAIRWAY, GOLGOTHA, and APHRODITE IX as well as handling the company's business affairs.

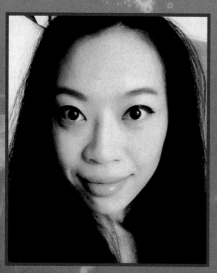

YISHAN LI

is a British/Chinese comic artist currently living in Shanghai. You can see a list of her projects at www.liyishan.com. Yishan Li has been drawing since 1998 and has been published internationally, including USA, France, Germany, Italy, and the UK. She has worked for publishers such as DC and Darkhorse and her last project was *Buffy: the high school years* graphic novels.

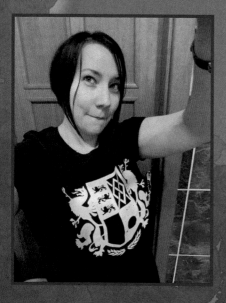

LINDA SEJIC

is a digital comics artist specializing in an expressive, dynamicart style. Her first major project with Top Cow was WILDFIRE, written by Matt Hawkins, which showcased her unconventional, character-focused technique and established her as an up-and-coming talent. Her critically acclaimed webcomic BLOODSTAIN is currently published in print from Top Cow, and is on its third volume. Linda lives in Croatia with her husband, illustrator Stjepan Sejic.

SEX ED

Welcome to Volume 2 of SWING! The first volume was more about Cathy and Dan's relationship with each other, this volume delves into actual swinging with couples, parties and club experiences.

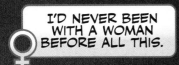

I'D NEVER BEEN WITH A WOMAN BEFORE ALL THIS.

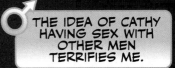

THE IDEA OF CATHY HAVING SEX WITH OTHER MEN TERRIFIES ME.

NARRATIVE

We have more of the his and her narrative boxes in this volume. I like narrative because it explores the space between what characters say and what they're thinking. As a writer, I find the differences there fascinating. In the first few drafts I wrote for this volume I had a LOT more narrative and I ended up stripping out most of it. It slowed the pacing down and was somewhat repetitive of what was shown in the art. Having the characters explain what we can clearly see in the artwork either by facial expression or the setting is a classic writer 101 fail.

Most of the narrative I kept was Cathy's. This is intentional as she is the one spearheading the lifestyle. It also is more about her journey and her trying to find a balance in her life.

FEMALE-LED SWINGING COUPLES MORE SUCCESSFUL

There are no hard statistics on this, but I've spoken and interviewed hundreds of swinger couples at this point and most of the longer-term ones have told me that the woman initiated the idea of it. What I included as the reasoning in the story is conjecture on my part. I really don't know. When I asked people why they never really had a good answer. It's a little less "skeevy" when the woman is on point though. That's not a great word to describe it, but I can't think of a better one.

DAN CHATTING PRETENDING HE IS CATHY

I won't out anyone, but I know someone who does this. He claims it makes him feel more comfortable about the guy and the whole experience. That line in the book where Dan talks about how he needs to like the guy for it to work is a real thing that I've heard from many male swingers in the couple.

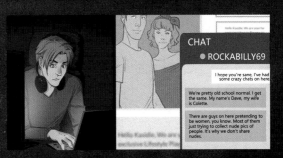

All the conversations Dan has on this page are actual conversations people shared with me.

SITUATIONS IN THIS BOOK REALISTIC?

The big debate about slice-of-life stories is always, are they realistic? Every swinging scene in this book, and all the fights the couple had as part of it, were either related to me by people or personally witnessed by me. There is always the eyewitness bias, but this is about as realistic as you can get...warts and all. I tried to show some of the emotional hurdles and problems people have embarking on this. Jealousy is a HUGE issue and springs up for people that have even been doing this for years. People do break up over swinging, but this is usually because they started doing it for the wrong reasons. The worst reason to swing is to try and salvage a relationship. These situations will magnify both the flaws and strengths of a relationship. It isn't for most people. If this is something you're interested in trying, take it slow and be open and honest about your thoughts and feelings. I had the characters say this in multiple places and almost stripped some of it out for repetitiveness but decided not to since it's so central and key to this whole lifestyle.

FAKES AND FLAKES

This is the number one complaint I hear from people in the lifestyle. I've never actually done online dating myself, so it could be very similar to issues people have with regular online dating...feel free to share your war stories on my Twitter or Facebook I'd love to hear them! The single dudes collecting pictures was one of the more fascinating things I came across. Some guys apparently have zero interest in meeting anyone but get off on getting these couples or the woman to share nude pics. This is dishonest so I categorize this as not consensual and is uncool. The flakes just don't show up or "ghost" people. I wonder if this is people that were fakes and decided to flake, but who knows. I've heard war stories about both.

SINGLE PEOPLE INTO COUPLES

This is a real thing and the unicorn title for single girls made me laugh so hard when someone explained it to me that I had to share it in the story. Every culture, hobby and subculture has its own language. It was interesting discovering the language of swinging. The unicorns, when real, are often women recently out of a long-term relationship and they are looking to have some fun without it being anything serious. So the key to them is to strike before they couple back up or you might miss a narrow window of opportunity.

COUPLES PLAYING APART

Some couples will play separately. This means the woman or man will hook up with a couple or other people as an individual even though they have a partner. Sometimes "partners" are not actually in a relationship but "friends with benefits" that seek out these kinds of encounters together. For a couple like Dan and Cathy, playing apart would never be an option and they would likely prefer couples in a longer-term relationship. Equal stakes is key. If they are both married or in a long-term relationship then they both have more to lose if things go bad or if anyone develops an emotional attachment. Sometimes emotional attachments are part of what people are looking for, but that's more polyamory or an open relationship. There is no cookie cutter way of doing this, every couple decides what their own boundaries are.

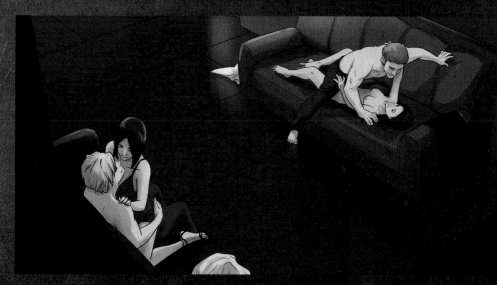

SWINGERS ARE NOT ASHAMED OF WHAT THEY DO

Part of the reason SWING and SUNSTONE are so successful is that the people who enjoy this type of lifestyle are not ashamed of what they do, and they support a sex-positive version of what they practice. I guarantee you know at least one swinger couple, but they'd never tell you unless they knew you wouldn't think less of them for it. Some lifestyle couples are very open about it and everyone knows. Others are secretive and keep that part of their lives compartmentalized. To each their own, whatever makes people happy is fine with me as long as it's consensual and doesn't involve animals, children or serious injury (or death).

FREQUENCY

How often do people swing? This is again couple-specific. I've met couples that do it as an annual thing just to scratch that itch. I've also met couples that do it every week and it's a way of life for them or a hobby. There are no easy answers to any of these questions so again, if you want to try this please take it slow and have LOTS of communication.

MY OTHER BOOKS

If SWING is the only book of mine you've ever read, thank you! I appreciate your support. Try one of my others, though. I've written so many. You can also read the first issues of many of our other books here for free to try them before buying:

https://topcow.com/comics/free-2/

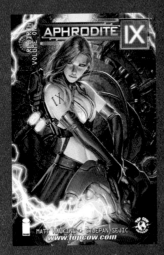
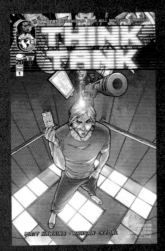
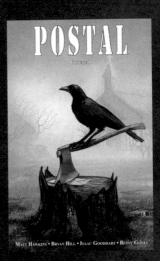

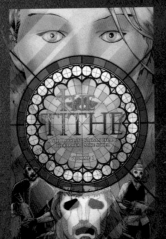
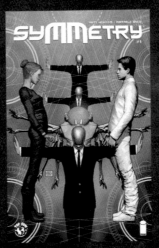

Thanks as always for reading my books and if you enjoyed this book please recommend it to a friend. You can reach me at any of my social media here if you have any questions, comments or want to relate a story you experienced.

Carpe Diem!

Matt Hawkins
Twitter: @topcowmatt | http://www.facebook.com/selfloathingnarcissist

Sugar

MATT HAWKINS
JENNI CHEUNG
YISHAN LI

LOVE COMES IN MANY FORMS

AVAILABLE NOW
IN TRADE PAPERBACK

6:48 AM 5TH STREET DOWNTOWN LOS ANGELES
LOU'S DINER
THERE'S NO RIGHT WAY TO MEET THAT SPECIAL SOMEONE.
LOU'S DINER
ALTHOUGH THERE ARE A LOT OF WRONG WAYS...TRUST ME.
I HAVEN'T HAD MUCH LUCK DATING HERE IN LA.
LOU'S
MY LAST BOYFRIEND BROKE UP WITH ME OVER TEXT.
JULIA

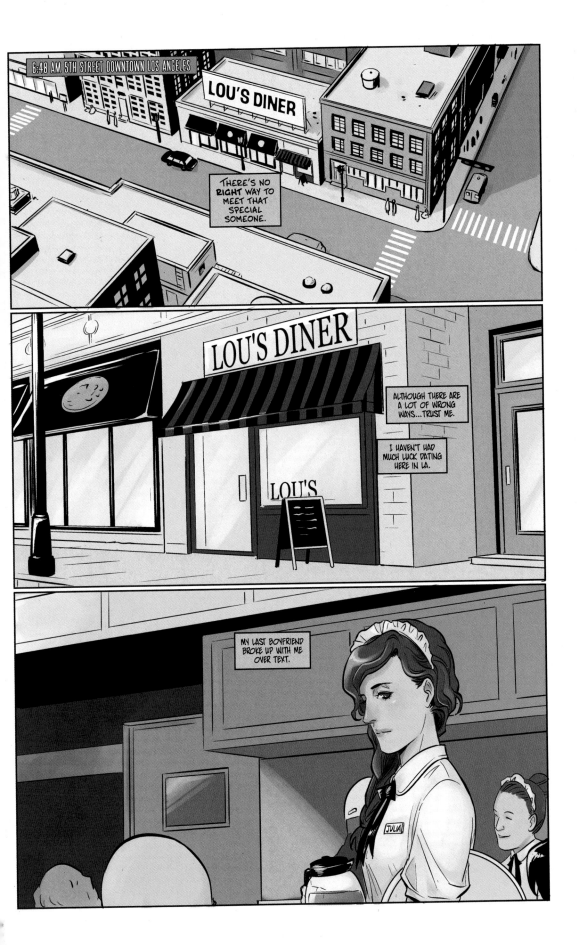

I WANT TO BELIEVE IN LOVE, LIKE THE SONG SAYS...BUT REAL LOVE AND WHAT WE SEE IN THE MOVIES AREN'T THE SAME THING.
THAT'S ENOUGH, THANKS, SWEETHEART.
JULIA
YOU MARRIED?
JULIA
JULIA.
NO.
BUT YOU ARE.
BURN, DUDE.
PICK UP THE CHECK, PLAYBOY. IT'S ALMOST SEVEN, WE'VE GOT TO GO.

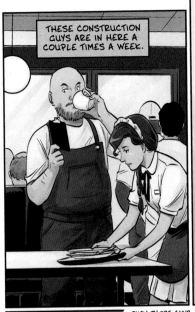

THESE CONSTRUCTION GUYS ARE IN HERE A COUPLE TIMES A WEEK.

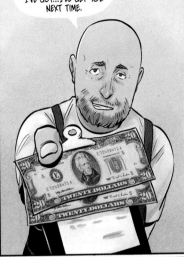

SORRY, SWEETHEART, DIDN'T KNOW THEY WERE STICKING ME WITH THE WHOLE THING. THAT'S ALL I'VE GOT...I'LL GET YOU NEXT TIME.

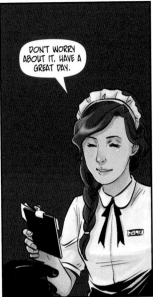

DON'T WORRY ABOUT IT, HAVE A GREAT DAY.

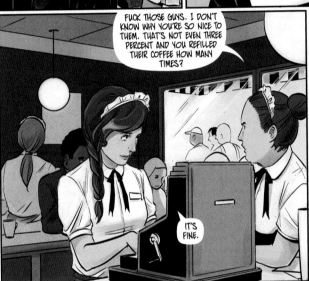

FUCK THOSE GUYS. I DON'T KNOW WHY YOU'RE SO NICE TO THEM. THAT'S NOT EVEN THREE PERCENT AND YOU REFILLED THEIR COFFEE HOW MANY TIMES?

IT'S FINE.

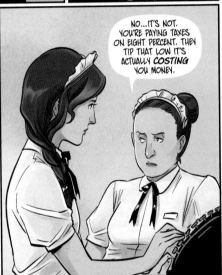

NO...IT'S NOT. YOU'RE PAYING TAXES ON EIGHT PERCENT. THEY TIP THAT LOW IT'S ACTUALLY *COSTING* YOU MONEY.

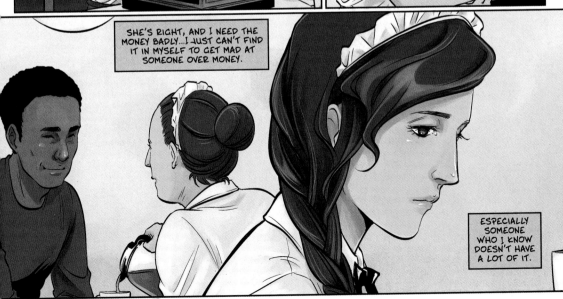

SHE'S RIGHT, AND I NEED THE MONEY BADLY...I JUST CAN'T FIND IT IN MYSELF TO GET MAD AT SOMEONE OVER MONEY.

ESPECIALLY SOMEONE WHO I KNOW DOESN'T HAVE A LOT OF IT.

YOU SHOULDN'T SIGN THAT, JOHN. AS YOUR LAWYER, I ADVISE YOU TO LET ME COUNTER.
IT'S A SHIT DEAL. WORST DIVORCE DEAL I'VE SEEN IN YEARS.
I JUST WANT TO GET IT OVER WITH...SO I CAN MOVE ON WITH MY LIFE.
MOVING ON? YOU CALL WHAT YOU'RE DOING MOVING ON? HAVE YOU EVEN LEFT YOUR HOUSE IN THE LAST WEEK FOR ANYTHING OTHER THAN WORK?

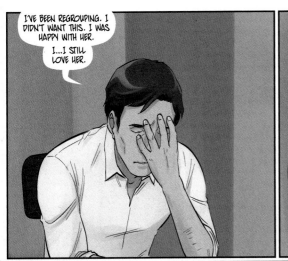

I'VE BEEN REGROUPING. I DIDN'T WANT THIS. I WAS HAPPY WITH HER.

I...I STILL LOVE HER.

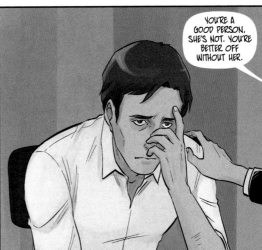

YOU'RE A GOOD PERSON, SHE'S NOT. YOU'RE BETTER OFF WITHOUT HER.

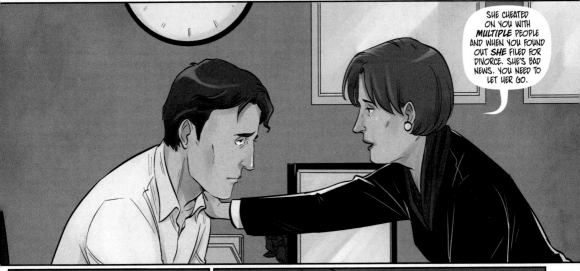

SHE CHEATED ON YOU WITH *MULTIPLE* PEOPLE AND WHEN YOU FOUND OUT *SHE* FILED FOR DIVORCE. SHE'S BAD NEWS. YOU NEED TO LET HER GO.

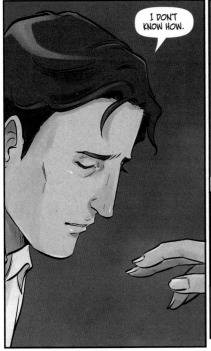

I DON'T KNOW HOW.

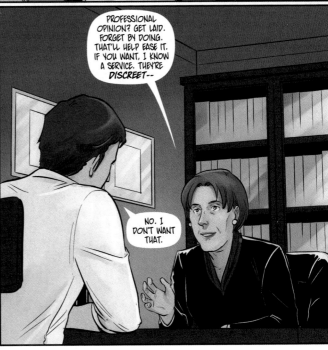

PROFESSIONAL OPINION? GET LAID. FORGET BY DOING. THAT'LL HELP EASE IT. IF YOU WANT, I KNOW A SERVICE. THEY'RE *DISCREET--*

NO. I DON'T WANT THAT.

11:00 PM
THESE MOVIES ARE ALWAYS SO UNREALISTIC.
OH, TREVOR, YOU FLEW ALL THIS WAY TO SUPPORT ME.
CHRISTY
I SHOULDN'T BE WATCHING THIS CRAP. I HAVE TO BE AT WORK IN SIX HOURS, I SHOULD BE SLEEPING.
YOU MUST REALLY LOVE ME.
I LOVE/HATE THESE MOVIES. I LOVE THEM FOR THE FANTASY...AND YEAH I GUESS I HATE THEM WHEN I REALIZE IT'S FANTASY. SIGH.
JULIA, I LOVE YOU SO MUCH.

SHHH, MY ROOMMATE IS PROBABLY ASLEEP.
I'M STEALTH MODE QUIET.
LIKE JAMES FUCKING BOND.
HOPE YOU LAST LONGER THAN SEVEN SECONDS, 007.
LET'S GO TO MY ROOM.

MY ROOMMATE CHRISTY IS A LITTLE MORE ADVENTUROUS THAN ME... ESPECIALLY WHEN SHE'S DRINKING.
IN A MINUTE.
SHE WOULDN'T DO THIS IF SHE KNEW I WAS AWAKE.
THUNK
THAT DIDN'T GET THEIR ATTENTION.
FWUMMP
FWUMMP
FWUMMP
OH!
OH

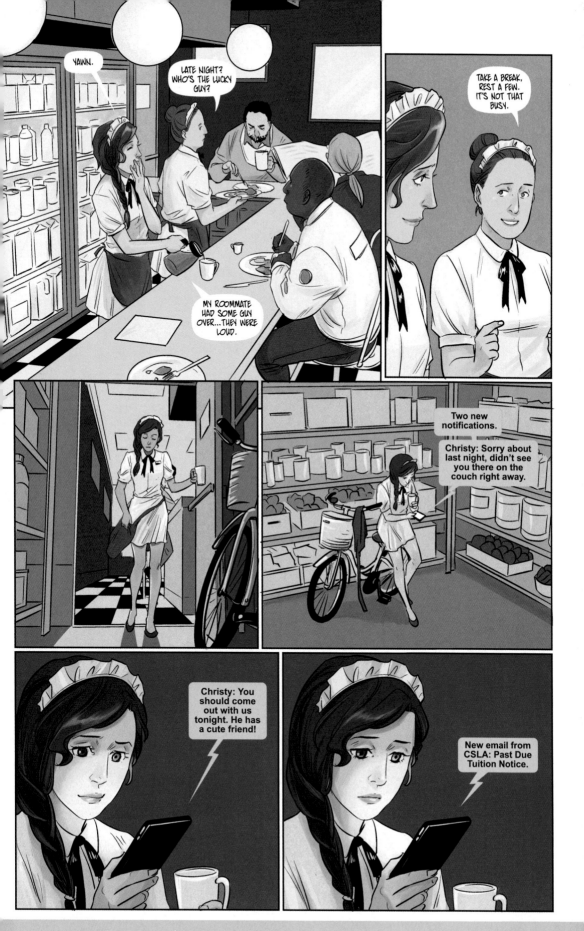

Continued in SUGAR Volume 1, AVAILABLE NOW

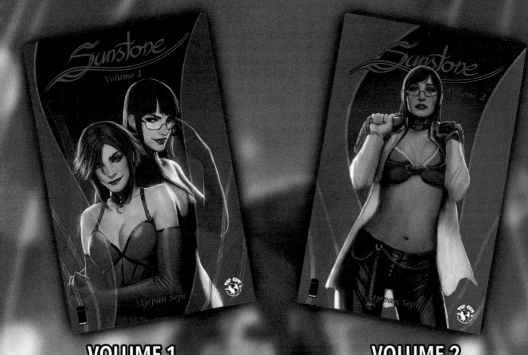

**VOLUME 1
DIAMOND CODE:
OCT140613**

ISBN: 9781632152121

**VOLUME 2
DIAMOND CODE:
FEB150538**

ISBN: 9781632152299

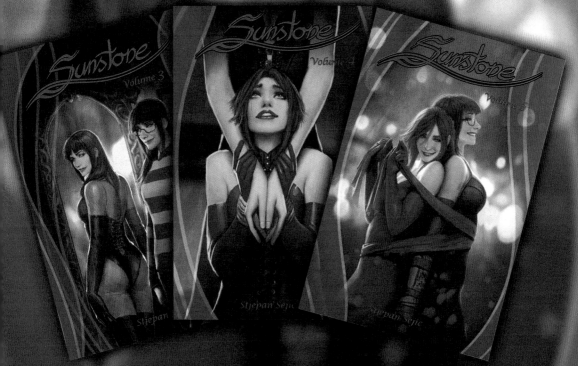

**VOLUME 3
DIAMOND CODE:
JUN150583**

ISBN: 9781632153999

**VOLUME 4
DIAMOND CODE:
OCT150579**

ISBN: 9781632156099

**VOLUME 5
DIAMOND CODE:
MAY160731**

ISBN: 9781632157249

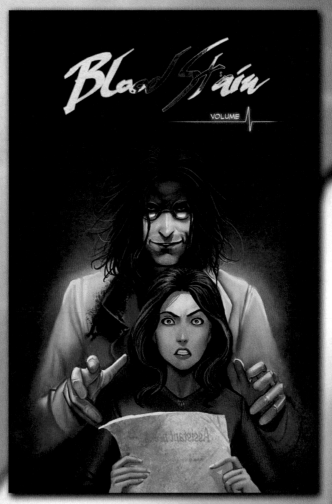

**VOLUME 1
DIAMOND CODE:
OCT150604**

Blood Stain
VOLUME
LINDA SEJIC
Blood Stain
VOLUME
VOLUME 2
DIAMOND CODE:
JUN160704
VOLUME 3
DIAMOND CODE:
AUG170621
ON SALE NOW!
image
TOP COW PRODUCTIONS, INC.
IMAGECOMICS.COM • TOPCOW.COM
FOLLOW #IMAGECOMICS #TOPCOW
Originally published on Deviantart by Linda Sej

Top Cow essentials checklist:

Aphrodite IX: Rebirth, Volume 1
(ISBN: 978-1-60706-828-0)

Blood Stain, Volume 1
(ISBN: 978-1-63215-544-3)

Bonehead, Volume 1
(ISBN: 978-1-5343-0664-6)

Cyber Force: Awakening, Volume 1
(ISBN: 978-1-5343-0980-7)

The Darkness: Origins, Volume 1
(ISBN: 978-1-60706-097-0)

Death Vigil, Volume 1
(ISBN: 978-1-63215-278-7)

Dissonance, Volume 1
(ISBN: 978-1-5343-0742-1)

Eclipse, Volume 1
(ISBN: 978-1-5343-0038-5)

Eden's Fall, Volume 1
(ISBN: 978-1-5343-0065-1)

The Freeze, OGN
(ISBN: 978-1-5343-1211-1)

God Complex, Volume 1
(ISBN: 978-1-5343-0657-8)

Infinite Dark, Volume 1
(ISBN: 978-1-5343-1056-8)

Paradox Girl, Volume 1
(ISBN: 978-1-5343-1220-3)

Port of Earth, Volume 1
(ISBN: 978-1-5343-0646-2)

Postal, Volume 1
(ISBN: 978-1-63215-342-5)

Sugar, Volume 1
(ISBN: 978-1-5343-1641-7)

Sunstone, Volume 1
(ISBN: 978-1-63215-212-1)

Swing, Volume 1
(ISBN: 978-1-5343-0516-8)

Symmetry, Volume 1
(ISBN: 978-1-63215-699-0)

The Tithe, Volume 1
(ISBN: 978-1-63215-324-1)

Think Tank, Volume 1
(ISBN: 978-1-60706-660-6)

Vindication, OGN
(ISBN: 978-1-5343-1237-1)

Warframe, Volume 1
(ISBN: 978-1-5343-0512-0)

Witchblade 2017, Volume 1
(ISBN: 978-1-5343-0685-1)

For more ISBN and ordering information on our latest collections go to:
www.topcow.com
Ask your retailer about our catalogue of collected editions,
digests, and hard covers or check the listings at:
Barnes and Noble, Amazon.com,
and other fine retailers.

To find your nearest comic shop go to: